DELIVER US FROM EVIL

BY
Linda K. Boutillette and Marilyn J. Burdett

Marilyn J. Burdett
Linda K. Boutillette

THIS BOOK IS BASED ON A TRUE STORY ACCORDING TO THE
FACTS AS WE FOUND THEM. TWO OF THE NAMES HAVE BEEN
CHANGED TO PROTECT THEIR INDIVIDUAL PRIVACY.

In spite of our investigative efforts, questions still remain unanswered.
In these circumstances reasonable judgments had to be made.

Dedication

With love we dedicate this book to our husbands Dave & Randy, who gave us constant support regardless of how bizarre our investigation became.

Philip Roy Publishers

c/o S.P.P.S.
150 Main Street
Spencer, Massachusetts 01562

Copyright © by L. K. Boutillette & M. J. Burdett 1992-1997
LIBRARY OF CONGRESS CATALOG CARD NUMBER - 97-92293

ISBN 0-9659272-0-2

ISBN 0-9659272-1-0

Printed in the United States of America

Editor
William J. Sweeney

Cover Design
Clifford Jette

10 9 8 7 6 5 4

In Memory of Maria Prouty

May Your Soul Rest In Peace

ACKNOWLEDGMENTS

Teddy Rabouin

Darlene Morse

Bobby Beaudin

Frank Marderosian - Background Investigators

Ernie Roberts

Christine Cournoyer

Bridget

PREFACE

We found it very difficult to accept the unexplained events and psychic phenomena that virtually haunted us during the research and writing of this story. Since we knew nothing about and didn't believe in the psychic world or past life regression, we struggled with our feelings to maintain a calm and reasoned perspective on normal day-to-day living. We had to confront and try to make sense of some very strange revelations and otherworldly dreams that made our lives quite uncomfortable. But after taking some time to learn how to look objectively at all the facts we uncovered, we can now finally chronicle these events.

The obituaries and newspaper articles remain in their unedited original form, just as they first appeared. You will also notice that many of these articles don't agree as to what actually happened here during the winter of 1899. There will be room for you to make your own speculations and draw your own conclusions, but there is no doubt this will be an unforgettable journey back in time, to a small New England town with a terrible secret.

THE DREAM

Linda's recurring nightmares were becoming more frequent and disturbing. Her husband, Dave, abruptly awakened by her uncontrollable cries, gently nudged her.

"Linda, it's okay, you're only dreaming," he consoled her. "Please don't cry."

From the blackness of night a bolt of lightning illuminated the bedroom, followed by a loud clap of thunder. The rumbling of the storm as it unleashed its fury added to the already unsettled mood surrounding the couple. It was enough to make them both sit up and take notice of what was happening.

Frightened by the storm and her nightmare, Linda cradled herself next to Dave.

"My God, I saw her again!" she gasped. He held her close as she began to describe her dream.

"It's the same nineteenth-century mansion I've seen a hundred times before." She paused to catch her breath and to feel the comfort of her husband's arms.

"A woman is standing at the top of the stairs, confused and terrified. Suddenly, she's running down the staircase, her long white nightgown cascading behind her. I feel the softness of her gown brush my arm as she runs past the parlor chair I'm hiding behind. The pounding of her heart echoes inside my head and I can sense her terror as if it were my own."

Dave shifted his body in an uncomfortable manner, trying not to be obvious.

"Please, Dave, hold me! ... if I can just talk this dream through, maybe between the two of us we can make some sense of it."

They had tried to sift through the details of Linda's nightmares before, with no success. This time, though, Dave felt much more urgency in her voice. Before she had a chance to ask if she was going out of her mind, he assured her she wasn't.

"God, I'm sorry to burden you with this. I just don't know what to do!" she admitted.

"You're doing the right thing just by talking about it. You don't want to keep this bottled up inside," Dave assured her.

A bit calmer she continued. "The sound of heavy footsteps reaches the bottom of the staircase. I hear the woman's chilling screams echo through the mansion as she attempts to escape. Everything is happening so fast. A man pushes her to the floor and is forcing himself on top of her. The weight of his body has already begun to force life's breath from her, when his two massive hands wrap themselves around her throat. In that split second her clear, ghostly eyes are staring into mine. She needs my help but it's too late. I squint in the darkness to get a glimpse of her killer, but the lengthening sunset shadows have cast a silhouette across the madman's face. And at this precise second it's as if I were frozen in time and then I wake up screaming. I feel like I'm linked to a hundred-year-old mystery or message ... and it will continue to haunt me until I figure out what it means."

The messenger in Linda's nightmares had also contacted someone else – someone whose life would be inextricably entwined with Linda's and Dave's and who would unwittingly participate in the most bizarre mystery of their lives.

Friday, 26 March 1990, dawned a spectacular early spring day in Spencer. Fat, fleecy-white clouds presided over the balmy breezes and warm sunshine. It was the kind of day that made folks dream of going for a drive with the top down, past lush green meadows, or hiking through forests of giant elm and oak. It was not the kind of day to be cooped up at work.

"How could you schedule a cleaning job on a day like this?" Dennis Meggett asked his business partner, Bobby Beaudin. "And the attic of the Prouty mansion of all things! Do you have any idea how big that place is? It'll take us all day!"

Bobby and Dennis's cleaning business had picked up sharply after the recent snows had melted. It felt good to be working regularly again, even in an attic on a day like this one. This was their first time at the Prouty estate, and the old house, like the name it bore, had stood for a very long time.

"I'd say we have our work cut out for us," Bobby said as they reached the top floor with their supplies. Several layers of dust covered everything in sight in the large attic room. Bobby opened the six gable windows to allow cross ventilation while they worked. The project was long, tedious and very dirty. At one point, the dust in the air became so thick, they needed to put on air filtration masks. Lunch was a welcome break.

"Find anything interesting down there in all that old furniture?" Dennis wanted to know.

"Yeah, there are lots of old photos and oil paintings, mostly of the same woman, a very beautiful woman. She's probably one of the Proutys. I wonder why the family didn't hold on to all this stuff?"

Bobby produced one of the old photos and showed it to his partner.

"I see what you mean. She's a knockout! When do you think it was taken?"

The back of the picture had a barely legible inscription:

"*Alfred Noyes Studio, Spencer, Mass., November 1898.*"

"She's really survived the last ninety years very well. I wonder who she is?"

Bobby brought out a box full of old books and loose documents.

"Take a look at this."

He blew the dust off what looked like an old manuscript and handed it to Dennis.

"What is it?" Dennis asked.

"I'm not sure, but from what I can tell, it looks like some kind of historical account of something that happened back then ... almost like a collection of news clippings. I think I'll take it home and read it tonight." He tucked the manuscript away in his bag.

Business took Meggett and Beaudin out of town the next few days. It wasn't until the following Tuesday evening that Bobby had a chance to put his feet up and relax. As he settled into his favorite chair, he suddenly remembered the document he'd brought home from the Prouty job. He got comfortable, turned to the first page and began to read.

From the very first word, Bobby began feeling the strangest sensation. He really couldn't put his finger on it – it was something between excitement and dread. Even his humble, sparsely furnished room seemed different. As his anxiety heightened he grew oddly cold. He then began to feel a sense of accomplishment ... as though he was taking care of some unfinished business.

After he read the final paragraph, he sat up straight and leaned his head back against the chair and carefully scanned the room. "What the hell am I looking for?" he said out loud. The lamp cast shadows on the wall giving the room a strange, unearthly look. "Maybe a walk around town will help calm me down."

The story had left an impression, cold, dark and disturbing. It had reached into his soul and taken hold. It would remain until he'd written some yet unknown ending.

When he returned from his brisk walk, he tried to sleep but visions from the past kept him fighting his pillow, distracting him from everything else but finishing McKenna's and McDonald's work. He decided the next step required him to talk about his discovery with two people he knew and trusted: his sister, Marilyn, and brother-in-law Randy.

Without a warning telephone call, Bobby armed himself with a hot cup of coffee and set out through the morning drizzle to Marilyn's. Both cars were in the driveway when he pulled in. It was now 7:00 a.m., Bobby opened the car door and began the short walk up to the house.

"What brings you out so early and on such a miserable day?" Marilyn asked with genuine surprise in her voice. "Are you okay? You look awful!" His drawn features betrayed his sleepless night. "I need a refill on my coffee before I explain why I'm here." He looked at her in a way she'd never seen before.

"This sounds serious, Bobby!" She walked over to the kitchen table and refilled his cup.

Randy joined them a moment later. "What's up, Bobby? It's a little early for you, isn't it?" Randy yawned as he poured himself a cup of the hot brew.

Bobby hesitated. "I'm not sure I can even put into words that you'll understand, what it is that's gotten hold of me. I don't know... you may think I'm crazy, but I want you two to be a part of this." He choked on the words.

"Part of what, Bobby?" Marilyn and Randy both asked at the same time.

"You're the only people I can trust with this. Please listen to what I have to tell you, then read this manuscript. I can't describe the feeling I have ... it's like life and death!"

His voice wavered as he began piecing together the whole story –from Henry's death, to McKenna's resignation, and all the high points in between. He became more animated as he recounted and developed McKenna's theories of how and why the murders took place.

"Bobby, it's just a story. Who knows what happened? You know what they say ... rumors and gossip are cherished until they become legend. It sounds like that is what's going on here. So please try to calm down." Without trying to mask her concern, Marilyn hesitated a moment before walking to the other side of the kitchen.

"Okay, okay, don't take my word for it, read this. I guarantee it will move you the same way it has me. This is a story that *must* be told. Please, work with me on this ... trust me." He set the manuscript down on the kitchen table. With some anxiety in his voice, and then looking them both in the eye, he added, "I sure hope you sleep better than I did after you've read it. Call me."

When he left he was most unsure if he'd convinced them.

That night, after dinner, Randy asked, "Aren't you the least bit curious?"

"About what?" Marilyn asked innocently.

"C'mon, you know what I'm talking about. The murder mystery your brother brought us this morning ... the historical account of all those deaths here in town a hundred years ago. What if this is the unsolved murder case of the century? Of *two* centuries?" Randy's curiosity was definitely piqued.

"Oh, I don't know, I suppose." Hers was definitely not.

"Well, it's time to find out what's gotten your brother so excited."

He picked up the manuscript and settled into the couch. The title grabbed his attention:

THE MOST AMAZING MYSTERY IN
THE NEW ENGLAND ANNALS

Marilyn sat nearby, occasionally peeking over to Randy. Finally she called, "Randy, 'Jeopardy!' is coming on! Give it a rest for a while."

Without a word, he waved one hand at her and continued the story. Good God, she thought, *he's becoming as obsessed as Bobby*. She decided to let him finish.

It was a while before he finally put the story down. He looked stunned. "This story is so evil, it makes the Watergate coverup look like a picnic in the park. I can't describe it to you in words that would make any sense. You've got to read it for yourself." He handed her the manuscript.

"I will, but not tonight. I'm really tired and I don't think I could stand the excitement."

Her sarcasm was lost on Randy, who was still back in 1899.

Randy woke many times that night to the voice of someone calling for help. There were no faces, no landmarks – nothing that would lend any sense of familiarity to the dreams. There was, however, an energy that seemed to be pulling him – no, more like inviting him – into what? It wasn't exactly a voice, either. It felt more like the energy from a light source, a hypnotic ray drawing him closer. The unfinished business and questions begged answers.

On a cold damp afternoon a few days later, Marilyn's curiosity finally got the better of her. It was time to read her brother's story. She had just reached the living room with a hot cup of chocolate, when the bright, late winter skies scudded over to the dark clouds of an approaching storm. It descended on Spencer in minutes and with tremendous ferocity. The wind picked up the freezing rain and drove it against everything manmade and natural. Electricity went out when one of the main transformers came crashing down in the middle of Route 9.

She hurried up to the spare bedroom to retrieve her kerosene lamp and a book of matches. There was plenty of fluid left in the bowl, and it reminded her of the many severe winter storms New Englanders had endured the last few years. She carefully brought the lamp downstairs, set it down on an end table and lit the wick. The lamplight was warm and welcoming. The scene was now perfect for a stormy afternoon of murder mysteries.

Before starting the story, she closed her eyes and tried to imagine what Spencer would have looked like in 1899. She pictured late fall, after the first frost had encouraged the trees to show off their brightest golds, crimsons and yellows. The streets were filled with the sights and sounds of a thriving and bustling small town, horsedrawn carriages proudly parading up and down Main Street, children laughing as they tumbled through piles of fallen leaves. The whole picture made her feel very much at home ... like she belonged there.

As the autumn winds blew stronger, the last of the summer leaves tried vainly to cling to their branches. A soft blanket of bright foliage now covered the gravel roads and wooden sidewalks. Warm afternoon sunshine gave way to colder nights and early morning frost.

Spencer was snuggled in a valley, surrounded by hills which had shed their mantle of summer greens in favor of a spectacular, but fleeting, fall mix. The Seven Mile River mirrored the blazing colors. Soon, all the rivers and ponds, which had been favorite swimming holes, would become playgrounds for ice skaters. Once the velvety white snow landed, the hardy outdoor folk would bring out their sleds, toboggans and ice-fishing gear and enjoy Mother Nature's wonderland.

Against the imagined backdrop of a Spencer she'd never known, Marilyn began her time travel back to a lovely, quaint, almost picture postcard perfect village.

The manuscript was lying exactly where she had left it, on the coffee table. She sat looking at it for a few seconds, then slowly leaned forward, picked it up and began reading about the plans for Henry and Iris's wedding. Every word drew her further into the complex web of deceit and murder, woven by a killer of unparalleled arrogance and cunning. It was almost beyond belief that Spencer could hold such diabolical secrets. She tried a few times to look away, to put it down, but couldn't. The extra layer of sweaters couldn't keep her from shivering as she read, turning the pages faster and faster. The subplots seemed to come from everywhere: history, lust, power, greed, incest, love and murder. It was almost impossible to digest everything in one reading.

ONE

In early January 1899, the small New England hamlet of Spencer, Massachusetts was making final preparations for the most extravagant and costliest wedding of the century. It was the union of a pair of young socialites from two of the most prominent families in the community.

Henry Hammond, at age twenty-three, was a tall, handsome and very striking figure of a man, and the only son of Ida and Aaron Hammond. Henry was about to marry his childhood sweetheart and the love of his life, Iris Prouty. Iris, charming, beautiful and well-educated, was a graduate of the prestigious Wellesley College in Boston. She was everything a man could desire in a woman. She had an angelic face framed by cascading long blond hair, a breathtaking beauty.

Henry's father Aaron, who had the same striking good looks as his son, had invested in real estate and owned a very successful wholesale beef business in town. Henry, his only heir, stood to inherit a considerable fortune.

The Proutys earned their success in the boot and shoe business. Iris's father William, along with his two brothers Fields and Merrick, owned and operated Prouty Brothers Shoe Manufacturing Company. William was a short, stout man with a stern look, a look that belied the button-popping pride he felt toward his daughter's upcoming wedding to Henry.

Yet there were some who did not share William's joyful anticipation. Foremost among them was William's wife, Maria. She went so far as to create an emotional scene at the Jennie Mendell dress shop. Mary Griffin, her seamstress, bore the brunt of Maria's outburst.

"I must find a way to stop this marriage ... it can never take place! "They will never be happy together!" Maria cried, anguish in her every word.

Mary was completely unprepared for Maria's furious reaction to what was going to be a joyous occasion. Mary reasoned that Maria's seeming overreaction stemmed from her recent deterioration of health.

Years earlier, Maria had been involved in a bizarre horse and buggy accident. Some accounts had intimated foul play led to Maria's fall. Others pointed to the fact that minor disasters had plagued Maria all her life, and this was just another in a long line. In any event, Maria, paralyzed on the left side of her body, faced a life of immobility and pain. In her youth she had been one of the most beautiful women in town. In addition to her stunning figure, her silky dark hair accented a complexion of pure ivory. However, the years since her fall saw her become old, frail and bitter.

Maria was not alone in her objections to the wedding. Curiously, Henry's father, Aaron, held serious reservations about his son's upcoming troth but kept them to himself until the appropriate time for him to act.

Thursday, January 5, was a particularly chaotic day at the Hammond meat packing company. The plant was buzzing, the workers in animated discussions about the strange disappearance of Frank Berry, one of their clerks. Berry had suddenly packed and left town unexpectedly, apparently without reason or explanation. It was a perplexing mystery that concerned Henry and also Albert Nichols, a close friend and confidential secretary at the plant. Henry, Albert and Frank were lifelong friends, so why on earth would Frank disappear without a word?

The First Congregational Church in Spencer as it looked at the time of the Prouty-Hammond case.

FIRST CONGREGATIONAL CHURCH

The wedding was scheduled for January 10 at the Congregational Church. That meant that if Aaron was to hatch a plan to sabotage his son's wedding, he had only five days to do it.

Shortly before 4:00 p.m., Albert was summoned to Aaron's private office. This was to be the most private of conversations, so Aaron made sure there were no witnesses. All who saw Albert leave the plant that day sensed that somehow the weight of the world had been placed on his shoulders, that he had been given a task so enormous he might collapse under its weight. Indeed he might, for Albert now had the awful responsibility of delivering a potentially explosive message to Henry, his dearest friend.

Albert was greeted at the Hammond front door by Anna Jensen, a lifelong family servant. He ignored her greeting and brushed past the elderly woman, into the grand foyer where Henry was descending the winding mahogany staircase.

"Since when do you leave your post before the end of the workday?" Henry said with a laugh. But his smile quickly faded when he saw the look of deep concern that clouded his friend's face. His youthful appearance was replaced with strain and his dark hair was mussed. "Albert, what is it? I've never seen you like this!"

Albert opened his mouth to speak but nothing came out. Henry reached the bottom of the stairs and slowly approached his friend.

"We've never kept anything from each other in all these years ... please talk to me!" Henry's voice was becoming more insistent.

Albert finally spoke. "I have a message for you from your father. He ordered me to deliver it immediately." His body noticeably shaking, he continued. "This is something I wanted no part of ... but I had no choice. To be frank, I don't believe there is anyone else who could do what I have to do now."

Henry was completely bewildered but recognized the need for a private conversation. He grabbed Albert's arm and led him upstairs to the sanctuary of his room.

Anna sensed the urgency of Albert's visit and felt left out of the family confidence. Her curiosity piqued to the point of exasperation. Outside Henry's locked bedroom door, Anna strained her ears only to hear the low muffled tones of unintelligible dialogue.

Sometime later when Anna had returned to her duties, she heard movement on the front stairs. Hurrying to the grand foyer, she only managed to glimpse the tail of Henry's waistcoat as the front door slammed behind him.

Much later, in the early hours of the morning, Henry returned to find Anna waiting for him with another message from his father. Aaron wished to speak directly to his son before they left the house the next morning.

Aaron made his way downstairs, through the kitchen. He took a lantern from the closet and cautiously guided himself outside into the cold morning darkness toward the stables. Henry was just minutes behind him. There were no cheerful greetings to Anna and Margaret as Henry darted through the kitchen and out the side door into the dark. The two maids crept to the kitchen window and peered out toward the stables, but all they could see was the lantern flame flickering across the horse stalls. Not a word or whisper passed between them as they tried to pick up the conversation between father and son. The eerie silence was soon shattered by angry shouts from both men. As Aaron's fierce anger grew, Henry's answers were shrilled and tortured. It was impossible to distinguish what was being said. As quickly as it started, the shouting stopped and the two maids were left to wonder what would happen next. Minutes passed like years and the silence became more unbearable than the shouting.

Finally, the door blew open and Aaron stormed in, muttering under his breath. He quickly passed through the kitchen and into the library. Anna glanced at the clock ... 5:55 a.m.

A few moments later Henry came in, looking pale and exhausted. His broad shoulders were slumped and he appeared dazed as he stumbled across the kitchen floor, following his father to the library.

The great old grandfather clock in the grand foyer began chiming 6:00 a.m., when suddenly an earsplitting explosion shook the house, canceling the last stroke of six. Anna and Margaret raced toward the open library door but stopped just before they reached it, clutching each other in terror. Very slowly they moved to the doorway. Aaron Hammond sat hunched over in his wing chair, still and unmoving. As they entered the room a curl of smoke greeted them, bearing the unmistakable odor of gunpowder. Margaret stood frozen, not able to move. Anna edged around Aaron toward the desk at the far wall. She stopped short and stood motionless.

There, at her feet, lay the lifeless body of young Henry Hammond, a bullet hole in his forehead and blood trickling down his cheek to the floor. Unable to speak, she fell to her knees beside the boy. Her hands went to her face as she began to weep uncontrollably over him. His sweet, innocent twenty-three years flashed before her – the twenty-three years she had cared for him as if he had been *her* son. How could he be gone?

It seemed like an eternity before Anna and Margaret could regain their composure. Once they came to their senses, they noticed a gun at Henry's feet – a Forehand and Wadsworth, .32-caliber revolver.

Anna's eyes scrutinized the room and came to rest on Aaron, still sitting in his chair hunched over in the same position. Finally, she heard him softly but desperately cry out, "Why? ... oh, God, why?" Great heaving sobs prevented him from saying anything else.

The business day began early in 1899 – factory whistles blew at 7:00 a.m. Though it was only 6:00, winter morning firelight glowed in most kitchens and smoke billowed from the chimneys as news of Henry Hammond's death spread throughout the small town.

At 7:00 a.m., Arthur Kingsley, the undertaker, arrived at the Hammond house along with his two assistants, Harry Jenks and Tom Clark, and a reporter from the *Worcester Telegram*, W. C. McDonald.

They were shown to the scene of Henry's death.

In a low voice, Kingsley said, "Let's get him upstairs ... and be careful not to touch the gun."

The four men lifted Henry's body out of the library, past his grieving parents, up to his room. They laid him on the bed and covered him. Kingsley briefly examined the body and surmised it was an obvious dead center shot, the result of a man turning a gun on himself. At that moment the medical examiner, Dr. Ephraim Norwood, arrived. After further examining the body, he confirmed Kingsley's suicide theory, then filled out the death certificate accordingly.

The darkness of that January morning shrouded the windows and filled the old house with shadows, as if it were mourning the passing of its favorite son.

Anna, still shaking, answered a knock at the front door. It was an old friend, Police Chief George McKenna. As soon as she saw him, Anna began to cry again. McKenna towered over the small woman as he took her into his arms and tried his best to comfort her.

George McKenna's experience in police science was very limited. He had little knowledge of ballistics, forensics or even fingerprinting. So the idea of opening a possible wrongful death case made him very apprehensive. Basic investigative procedure told him to begin questioning Aaron. But the elder Hammond, head in his hands, was still unable to speak. He could only nod his head toward the doorway

McKenna then called McDonald, the *Worcester Telegram* reporter.

"I want you to show me exactly where the body was found," McKenna asked.

As they entered the library, McDonald pointed to the blood stain on the floor. "His head was there, feet over there, near the desk."

"And what about the gun ... where was it?" the chief continued.

The reporter indicated the spot.

"It was right next to his feet."

They both searched the entire area around and under the desk, but the revolver had disappeared.

"It *was* there, I'm telling you! We all saw it!"

McDonald's face, now as red as his hair, was becoming quite agitated.

"Calm down," the chief told him, "I'm sure it will turn up."

In spite of his overt confidence, McKenna was beginning to have doubts of his own.

McDonald added, "Maybe Jenks or Clark picked it up, although Mr. Kingsley specifically told us not to touch it."

All of a sudden this was not becoming a simple case of suicide, neatly wrapped up by the undertaker and medical examiner. The chief didn't want to consider the enormous ramifications and political fallout in his jurisdiction if a wrongful death could be proved and linked to the Hammond name.

The two men went upstairs.

"Does anyone know where the gun went to?" McKenna asked.

"What gun?" asked the doctor. "I didn't see a gun at the death scene. I stopped there first before I came up here."

"But it was there when we moved the body," Kingsley insisted. "I stepped over it and told the men not to touch it."

McKenna went back downstairs to question Jenks and Clark. Their story supported Kingsley's in every detail. They both insisted they had seen, but had not touched the weapon. Confused and frustrated with this new mystery, the chief went back upstairs where Kingsley and Dr. Norwood continued to work on the body.

"Are you sure this was a suicide?" McKenna's voice was noticeably louder.

"Of course I'm sure," the doctor retorted. "It was a dead-center shot."

"Could anyone else have scored as clean a target?" asked the chief.

"He could, provided Henry would stand still long enough to let him do it," the doctor replied sarcastically.

The chief decided not to dignify the doctor's last remark with a comment, but rather give serious thought to some of the homicide aspects of the case. There was no question that the gun was the key piece of evidence and must be found immediately, so he renewed his search beginning in the library. With painstaking precision, McKenna searched every inch of the house. By late afternoon, he'd not only *not* found the gun, but was unable to interview the grief-stricken family and servants.

Since there was very little more he could do at the Hammond estate, he decided to return to his office, still puzzling over the missing gun and any motive someone would have to use it on Henry. On his way back he decided to stop at the medical examiner's office.

"Anything conclusive yet, Ephraim?" McKenna asked.

"Nothing so far, George. This case has certainly taken an incredible turn. Any luck finding the gun?"

"That's the strangest part of all. How could something as obvious as a .32-caliber revolver simply vanish? I'm afraid all I have now is questions ... no clues and no answers."

"Well, you know there will be a lot of folks around here who are going to *want* some answers. I sure wouldn't want to be in your shoes!"

"Thanks for the vote of confidence, Ephraim. When can I see that medical report?" McKenna headed for the door.

"I'll have it for you first thing in the morning. Good night."

"Thanks, doctor. I'll see you tomorrow."

With that, he walked the few blocks back to his office.

The chief was sitting alone at his desk. It was a few minutes after 6:00 p.m. when one of the local schoolboys rushed in, completely out of breath.

"Chief, Chief! Come quick, please hurry!" The young man could barely get the words out.

"Hey, Daniel, take it easy. Slow down and tell me what's got you so excited." McKenna tried to calm the boy.

"Chief, you've got to come quick. They've just found Mrs. Prouty ... she's dead!"

The news was like receiving a tremendous blow to the side of his head. Now suddenly McKenna was having trouble catching his own breath. He quickly threw down his paperwork and raced over to the Prouty house, young Daniel hard on his heels. Both McKenna and McDonald arrived at the same time. News traveled like lightning in Spencer, so it was no surprise that an old family friend, Dr. Norwood, had already arrived.

"Ephraim, what happened here? How did she die? Who found the body?" The chief's questions flew at the doctor.

Norwood, who had just suffered the loss of two close family friends in the same day, was completely overwhelmed. He somehow felt that the arrival of the police and the growing group of reporters was an invasion of Prouty family privacy. And in spite of the newest tragedy, he wanted them all to disappear so he could personally console the grieving family.

After the chief's barrage of questions, the doctor raised his hand, his dark eyes portrayed a cold stare before he responded.

"I'm first going to consult with the family, after which I will answer your questions as best I can."

The chief tried to get a quick question in but the doctor had already turned and left for the drawing room where the surviving Prouty family members were assembled.

Sometime later, when Dr. Norwood returned, he announced he would act as their spokesman.

"I've given Mr. Prouty a mild sedative to help him rest. He can't see anyone now, much less answer any of your questions. Iris, who just this morning lost her fiancé, collapsed earlier. She is resting. The servants have been given part of the day off and have not yet returned."

The doctor continued.

"Maria has been ill for some time. Since she was under my care, doctor-client privilege prevented me from revealing her condition. She died from complications of heart disease, no doubt induced by the shock of Henry Hammond's death this morning. Her husband found her at approximately 6:00 p.m., after he'd returned home from work. He found her in the attic once he had searched the rest of the house."

Dr. Norwood's cold and oddly calculated reading of the facts surrounding Maria's death seemed to point to a much more sinister scenario. To Chief McKenna, again there were many more questions than answers.

Why were *all* the servants given the afternoon off, he wondered. It seemed unlikely that the entire staff would be off at the same time, leaving the family alone. And how did such a sick and frail woman make her way up three flights of stairs to the attic? And what could she have been doing in that unheated attic, alone, after dark, on a cold January night? What of Dr. Norwood's *cold reading* of the facts? It reminded McKenna of lines that had been scripted. What more does the good doctor know? There seemed to be no end to the questions.

It was as if Norwood had read the chief's mind. Before he knew it, the doctor quietly escorted him into the study and closed the doors behind them.

"I sent those reporters on a wild goose chase," the doctor slowly began.

"What are you talking about?" McKenna was more confused than ever.

"I told them, and you, that Maria died from complications of heart disease ..." the doctor said, barely able to get the words out. "I believe Maria Prouty strangled herself with a man's silk muffler."

"Strangled herself?"

The notion began to resemble the wildest fiction.

"Are you saying she hanged herself from an attic rafter with a scarf?" McKenna was becoming more confrontational.

"You're the family spokesman, what has Mr. Prouty said? After all, he found her. What evidence is there she committed suicide?" McKenna insisted.

"He found her on the floor with a muffler wrapped tightly around her neck. What else could have happened?" Norwood almost sounded apologetic.

"Please, Doctor, I want to see for myself. Show me where he found her!"

In silence they climbed the stairs to the third floor. When they had reached the top of the last staircase, McKenna turned the door handle and gave a push. It resisted. He put his shoulder to it and pushed much harder. It finally opened. The attic room was cavernous, damp and very cold. Huge vaulted beams and timber trusses were firmly set in place to support the great weight of its roof. It all gave the interior the look of a fourteenth-century castle. It also made McKenna very uneasy. He buttoned the top button of his coat and pulled up his collar. He felt the hair rise at the nape of his neck. His broad shoulders slumped forward as Doctor Norwood preceded him to the area of open floor where Maria's body was found.

"Right here," he pointed out. "She was lying right here."

"If she was hanged, what was she doing on the floor?" McKenna asked.

"Mr. Prouty couldn't leave her like that," Norwood replied.

McKenna looked up from the spot, searching for a hook, spike or joist that could have supported Maria's dying body. He saw none. Nor were there any other signs of a disturbance in the otherwise orderly attic. The trunks, boxes and old furniture were stacked neatly along the walls. Nothing seemed out of place, and there was nothing that he could see which could have assisted Maria to climb to her death.

As the evidence for suicide became weaker in the chief's mind, his foul-play theory was gaining more and stronger credibility. If this death *was* murder, he had the weapon but no motive. The doctor interrupted his thoughts.

"George, I'm going back to my office. I'll be available to talk more about this later."

"Are you still sticking to suicide in your examiner's report?" the chief asked.

"With the lack of any other solid evidence, yes. This isn't an exact science, George. I work with what I've got. I'll be leaving soon. Are you coming?"

"No, not right now, Ephraim. I still need to find a few more pieces to this puzzle. Good night."

"Good luck and good night!" the doctor called out as McKenna left.

Eighteen hours after Henry Hammond's death and six hours after Maria Prouty's, the chief found himself at Arthur Kingsley's morgue. Under the cold white electric light, Maria Prouty's emaciated body lay face down on a zinc table. As he looked at her, he felt a sense of revulsion at the way she died but also the exhilaration of a challenging investigation. He was becoming more and more convinced that he had seen the results of two murders today.

Although forensic medicine was not McKenna's area of expertise, he couldn't help noticing a purple bruise between the shoulders on Maria's back. Norwood did not mention this in his report, but how could he have missed it? The report *did* mention a bruise on the left temple. There was no discoloration, however. The chief decided Maria had either fallen against a heavy object or had been hit by one. Other bruises got his attention, too. What about the shallow scratches on the forehead, cheek and bridge of the nose? Why were these omitted from the examiner's report? All these injuries must have occurred before the strangulation, otherwise there would have been more signs of a struggle. Finally, McKenna noticed a few tiny wood splinters under her upper lip and fingernails. He was now positive that Maria Prouty was a victim of homicide.

After reviewing the examiner's report and listening to Chief McKenna's dissenting testimony, Judge Hill, along with Deputy Sheriff Henry Draper, decided to let stand Dr. Norwood's report. In spite of this setback, McKenna pressed on with his own investigation.

Life in Spencer was beginning to return to normal. Aaron Hammond arrived at his meat packing plant at 6:00 a.m., Friday morning, January 13. It was his first day back to the plant since he'd buried his son. It was an unusually busy morning and since they were still shorthanded, Aaron immediately noticed Albert had not yet arrived. He called for Martin Maynard, one of his assistant managers, to hitch up a team of horses and ride out to the Nichols house in East Brookfield, just outside of Spencer, to find Albert.

Martin H. Maynard, calling to take Albert Nichols to his work, Martin H. Maynard made a shocking discovery.

In the cellar of this house, the body of
Hammond's confidential clerk was found.

Martin reined in his horses in front of the large and beautiful Nichols home. At that hour, he could see a flickering light shining from the kitchen through the winter darkness. He went to the side door and knocked. There was no answer. He looked through a window, straining his eyes to see any sign of movement. There was a faint beam of light coming from what looked like the entrance to the cellar stairs. He let himself in, moving slowly toward the door.

"Hello!" he called out hoarsely. Silence ... not even an echo.

Martin stepped through the doorway and descended the stairs one careful step at a time. He held his lantern out in front of him and peered into the inky darkness. He was suddenly very cold – a bone chilling cold where the added chill factor is fear. He felt his way along a stone wall, smelling the musty odor of the damp earthen floor. The smoke from his oil lamp cast eerie dancing shadows on the old wooden beams, adding to his growing sense of dread. He paused for a moment and listened. But there was only silence, and the only sound he could hear was his pounding heart. There was something very wrong here, he thought.

Halfway across the floor he stopped and looked down. He was standing in a shallow pool of blood! He was so terrified, he lurched forward only to trip over something in his path. He lowered the lantern and was face to face with a dead Albert Nichols. Martin quickly backed away, his left hand over his face. When he opened his eyes he was able to look more carefully at the body. There appeared to be a severe gash to the throat that had bled profusely. It was most likely caused by the straight razor lying near Albert's head. Martin then noticed a piece of paper clutched in the young man's hand. At this moment events began to disconnect for Martin. Disobeying every rule of common sense he'd ever learned, he bent down and picked up the bloody note. As he began to examine it, he was overcome with dizziness and nausea from the smell of death and the hideous texture of the bloody paper. Unable to read it, Martin dropped the note to the floor, turned, and hurried up the stairs to the kitchen. He stopped at the sink to wash Albert's blood from his hands, then splashed cold water on his face.

Martin understood his responsibility for waking Albert's parents and telling them the awful news. He stood for a moment in the kitchen, collecting his thoughts. What an incredible tragedy that this young man, a dear friend blooming with life, now laid unmercifully butchered. Could Albert have taken his own life or was this a planned scene to mask murder with the appearance of suicide.

When he left the house, Bert and Sarah Nichols, Albert's parents, were collapsed in each other's arms, grieving.

Martin grabbed the reins and sent the team of horses plunging down the road to the office of East Brookfield Deputy Sheriff, Warren Tarbell. The deputy immediately sent for McKenna and notified Kingsley, the undertaker. When Chief McKenna arrived, the two officers questioned Martin thoroughly, then left for the Nichols home. Again, the undertaker had arrived before the police, and again had removed the body for Dr. Norwood's examination.

"How do you account for his death?" McKenna asked Kingsley.

"A deep cut in the side of the throat severed the carotid artery, probably caused by the straight razor we found next to the body. I've seen it before," the undertaker replied. "But I will leave the exact circumstances of his death to Doc Norwood."

"Has anything else in the cellar been disturbed?" the chief asked.

"No ... everything is still exactly as we found it." Kingsley seemed to be getting anxious. "We didn't touch a thing."

"We?" McKenna wondered aloud.

"Yes ... me and my helper, Tom Clark" he reminded him.

"Oh, yes, Tom." The chief recalled. "I'll see you back at your office once the medical examiner's report is finished. By the way, Kingsley, Martin told us he found Albert holding a bloodstained note. What did you do with it?"

"We didn't see a note," Kingsley admitted. "Nor did Bert or Sarah. Everything is just as it was when we got here."

The chief turned to Deputy Tarbell.

"Let's check the cellar."

The two detectives descended the cellar steps as though they were approaching a tomb. The acrid odor in the cold, damp air grimly reminded McKenna of two other recent deaths, and whose mysteries were far from being solved.

McKenna began at one end of the room, Tarbell the other. As they moved toward each other, they covered every square inch of the cellar floor, finding the razor, blood stains and signs of a struggle in the damp earth, but no note. Physical evidence just doesn't vanish, the chief surmised. Another wave of frustration came over him as he tried to reconcile the statements of witnesses who had discovered the recent deaths and the investigators and support staff who followed. Could it be that those original witnesses were so shocked at what they saw that they *imagined* seeing evidence that wasn't really there? What other possible explanation is there?

McKenna and Tarbell returned to their respective offices to file their reports. In the meantime, preparations were being made for yet another funeral in Spencer.

At home that evening, McKenna was rereading the *Worcester Telegram* accounts of the Hammond-Prouty suicides.

Special to the Telegram

> *Spencer, Jan. 6 — With everything to make life*
> *worth living, with no apparent motive in sight, Henry*
> *Hammond, only child of Aaron Hammond and*
> *wife, shot himself in the forehead at 6 o'clock*
> *this morning at the fine residence of his parents,*
> *27 High Street.*

Startling sequel to the Hammond suicide

> *There are no new developments in the two tragic*
> *events at Spencer. The town, shocked by the*
> *self-inflicted death of Henry Hammond Friday,*
> *was startled again by the news of the death*
> *of Mrs. William H. Prouty, the mother of Miss*
> *Iris Prouty, Mr. Hammond's fiancee. Mrs.*
> *Prouty had been in poor health for some time and*
> *was undoubtedly overcome by the tragedy of*
> *Friday, which affected her daughter so closely.*
> *She took her own life by strangulation .*

Undoubtedly, the chief thought sarcastically. Is this an account of what really happened? He put the paper down and shook his head, never imagining the events surrounding these two deaths would be disregarded so quickly and easily. He leaned his head back, closed his eyes and began mulling over the facts again. He was soon asleep.

A week passed, and life in Spencer seemed to proceed normally, at least on the surface. Beneath the calm exterior of business-as-usual, the specter of recent tragedy hung motionless over the town like an ominous dark shadow. The town had been visited by another violent death more gruesome than the last, and still more strangely, at the exact hour of six.

Aaron Hammond's cold storage meat business was thriving, but serious delivery problems loomed on the horizon if Hammond couldn't resolve his staff shortage. He recruited a young French Canadian, George Dumas, who lived nearby in what was known as Upper Wire Village, a settlement near the large Wickwire Steel Company. Dumas had always been known in town for his cheerful, outgoing personality. That all seemed to change once he'd signed on at Hammond's. A sense of gloom and dread clouded over him along with a severe apprehension of what might come from his connection to the Hammond family. He confided his fears to his friend, Alec Boulay, who dismissed them as the result of idle gossip.

"If I didn't need this job so badly, I'd never work for the Hammonds," Dumas confessed. "I wake up in the middle of the night and I hear Henry calling me. Then I answer him ... 'I'm coming'!"

"Forget that nonsense, George. Go home and get yourself together," Boulay encouraged his friend. "This job is a great opportunity for you to get on with your life."

That evening at the Cabana Saloon, Dumas told everyone that he felt he was going to die. The declaration took everyone's breath away. Although his friends all gathered around to try to make him feel better, no amount of alcohol or the encouragement of well-meaning comrades could allay the fear that welled up in him. Against their protests, he told them he was going to get a gun to protect himself. He told them that there was an evil around him and that he was not going to suffer the consequence of Henry Hammond or Albert Nichols.

Early the next morning, Friday, January 20, Chief McKenna received an urgent message to get right over to the Dumas home. When he arrived, George's wife, Selina, was standing outside the woodshed, sobbing into her apron. She pointed toward the woodshed door. The chief pushed it open. The gray, unforgiving morning light revealed the lifeless body of George Dumas, lying on the earthen floor with a bullet hole directly in the middle of his forehead. McKenna staggered a few steps backward and slumped against the shed wall, his hands to his face. It was becoming increasingly more difficult to maintain his composure in the face of such carnage, much less conduct investigations and solve the mysteries.

The chief did have something to be thankful for – Kingsley hadn't arrived yet to move the body. He imagined everything was just as it was when the "murder" took place. McKenna closed his eyes and tried to recreate the crime as it might have happened.

Early that morning, Dumas quietly went out to the woodshed to clean and load the pistol he'd bought the night before. His attacker completely surprised him, knocked him to the floor, clamped a hand over his mouth, and shot him in the forehead, using Dumas's own gun! His attacker fled ... to where? Neighbors from both sides came running when they heard the shot, and Mrs. Dumas had a clear view of the shed and the back yard. Whoever it was would have been seen. And what about the gun? If his attacker wanted this to look like suicide, why did he take the revolver?

McKenna's investigative ledger was overbalanced with questions and precious few conclusive answers. Kingsley and Norwood hadn't arrived yet, so the chief decided to go over the crime scene once more to see if he'd missed anything. He began at the back of the 12'x14' structure, checking every square foot for any kind of clue. No gun, no suicide note. Of course there's no suicide note, he reasoned. Why would a man who was terrified of being murdered take his own life? He added this to the growing list of questions. Four violent deaths within a month. There had to be someone or something at work here. McKenna had to find the connection.

Kingsley and Norwood arrived in time to find the chief still lost in his thoughts. He showed them the death scene, then went inside to try speaking with the grieving widow.

Since it was Selina Dumas who had discovered her husband's body, McKenna again had access to an original witness who could describe the scene with firsthand knowledge.

"Selina, I know this is very difficult, but I must ask you some questions about what's happened here..." his voice trailed off. "I have to know what happened to the gun that killed George."

"Chief McKenna," her voice trembled, "I begged him not to get a gun, but he went out last night anyway. I don't know if he bought one because I didn't see him after he left ... not until this morning when I found him." She began to cry again.

"When you found him, was there any sign of a gun on or near him?" he asked softly.

"No, I didn't see anything but the body of my dead husband." She could barely speak. "I hadn't seen him all night and was very worried. As a matter of fact, I was thinking of coming to see you, about him being missing. I was working in the kitchen, around 6:00 a.m., when I heard a loud crash that sounded like it came from the shed. I took my lantern and ran outside. The neighbors from both sides were running to meet me. When we met at the shed door, I opened it and saw him lying there. That's when I passed out. They sent someone to fetch you and, well, you pretty much know the rest."

"Do you have any idea why George felt he needed a gun?"

"Since he got his new job, he felt threatened by some evil that seemed to be following the Hammond family. He wanted something to protect himself with ... at least this is what I heard from some of the folks who were at the Cabana Saloon last night. He never did talk to me much about things that worried him. I wish he had."

She took a moment to catch her breath and continued.

"You know, Chief, there's something else. George went to Worcester yesterday afternoon to meet with someone who is working for, or has worked for, Aaron Hammond. When he came home he was very upset and wouldn't talk to me. Without even a bite of dinner, he went directly to the Cabana to see Alec Boulay. That's the last time I saw him alive."

McKenna left Selina Dumas to grieve, comforted by some of her women friends from next door. He was filling out his police report when Dr. Norwood walked into his office.

CHARLES DUMAS

"Have you finished your examination, Ephraim?" The chief was almost afraid to guess what the answer might be.

"Yes, I have, George, but I'm afraid you're not going to like it," the doctor replied sternly. "Suicide."

"You can't be serious!" McKenna shouted. "Are you telling me that a man who confesses to a barroom full of his friends that he's afraid to die, that he's going to get a gun to *protect* himself, turns around twelve hours later and puts that same gun to his *own* head and pulls the trigger? Even you would have to agree it's preposterous. He was murdered, Doctor, just like all the others. And I would like it very much if you would open your eyes long enough to see that and maybe even help me prove it!" The chief was now screaming.

"I'm not going to stand here and listen to your ranting, George. I have filed my report. Based on my findings, it was suicide. Goodbye."

With that, the doctor quickly left.

"This is just plain bullshit," the chief muttered to himself after his office door had closed. "Someone is building a wall of conspiracy around this case and I'll be damned if I'm going to let them prevent me from getting to the bottom of these murders."

The collective nerves of Spencer's townsfolk had become frayed to the point of tearing apart. There were many superstitious people who believed that a more aggressive investigation would cause more tragic deaths. Others supported Chief McKenna's conviction to finish the job he started, in spite of possible recriminations from local influential families. The newspapers were doing their best to fan the flames of hysteria among the townspeople by printing sensational pieces that were marginally true, misquoting sources and making glaring typographical errors. Unfortunately, there was nothing McKenna could do about that.

On 27 January 1899 another Friday dawned. The chief was trying to put all the newspaper rantings and hysterical citizens out of his head for a while, and just enjoy breakfast at the Massasoit Hotel. It was to be a very short meal.

"Chief McKenna! There you are," McDonald, the *Worcester Telegram* reporter, called out across the hotel dining room. "I've been looking all over for you." Out of breath, he continued. "We've got to go to Worcester. They've just found John Taylor, one of Hammond's salesmen, with his throat slashed! C'mon, hurry!"

They both ran out of the hotel to a buggy and team of horses that McDonald had ready for them. On the way, McKenna questioned the reporter.

"Who found the body?"

"Taylor had been staying with a friend in Worcester, a fellow named John Paquette. He found Taylor's body," McDonald answered.

"How about signs of a struggle or a weapon at the scene?"

The chief again sensed a new wave of answerless questions.

"I don't know, Chief, but you'll have a chance to talk to Paquette as soon as we get there. He should be able to tell us something."

The reporter gave an extra crack to the reins. His horses responded with an added burst of speed.

By the time they reached Paquette's Millbury Street address in Worcester, John Taylor was already dead. The local authorities had arrived but not the medical examiner, so the body and any physical evidence remained exactly where they had fallen, or so McKenna hoped.

After introducing himself to the police investigators, he explained a possible connection between Taylor's death and the other so-called suicides in Spencer. He was then given permission to conduct his own independent investigation.

"What time did you discover the body?" the chief began questioning Paquette.

"I was awakened a little after 6:00 a.m. when I heard a heavy thud on the floor upstairs. I immediately ran up to see what had happened. I knocked on John's door several times, then opened it myself."

Paquette spoke in very slow, halting phrases. He paused for a moment as though he were remembering each ghastly detail.

"What did you see?" McKenna persisted.

"I saw John's body lying face up on the floor, blood coming out of a terrible gash in the side of his throat and pouring onto the carpet. There was a straight razor lying by his left shoulder."

Paquette was now on the verge of tears as he continued.

"We had known each other for years, and he was my best friend. How could he kill himself?"

"We haven't established his death was a suicide, Mr. Paquette. That will be determined by a police investigation and the medical examiner's report."

Thank God we're out of Norwood's jurisdiction, McKenna thought.

"Is there any reason you can think of why Mr. Taylor would take his own life?"

"I'm not sure ... but last Thursday he had a meeting here in town with one of his friends and co-workers from the Hammond plant. When he returned he wouldn't talk about it with me. And furthermore, he seemed very depressed ... more so than I've ever seen him before. I wish I could tell you more."

"You've been a great help, Mr. Paquette. I'm sorry to have burdened you with these questions so soon after your tragic loss. I want to help in any way I can. If there's anything else I can do, please let me know."

"Just give me a little time right now." Paquette turned and went back to his room.

McKenna recalled his interview with George Dumas's wife, Selina. She mentioned a meeting her husband had in Worcester the previous Thursday. Could he have met with John Taylor? But why? How did they know each other? He began juggling a new series of questions. His instinct told him that some of them were about to be answered.

The next day, the chief received a request to meet Judge Hill in his chambers as soon as possible.

"Good morning, Your Honor." He took a seat across the judge's desk. "You sent for me?"

"Yes, George, it's about these recent suicides." The old jurist looked up to catch the look on McKenna's face. "I think it's time we put them to rest. Further investigation is just a waste of time."

The arrow hit home.

"It hasn't been a waste of time for me to come up with incontrovertible evidence that the five deaths in the past three weeks were murders, Judge!" McKenna replied. His conspiracy theory hung like a cloud over his head, but he wasn't prepared to accuse anyone yet, let alone argue with a well-respected local judge.

"Circumstantial evidence, George. In some of these cases there's either no weapon, or no sign of a struggle, or no motive. There is no reason why anyone would want to kill all these people. You and your scandal-mongering newsmen should just let this whole thing go away." Judge Hill was clearly becoming irritated.

"The people of Spencer have a right to know what's going on, and I'm going to find out for them," McKenna insisted.

"Listen, Chief, Deputy Draper and Dr. Norwood are positively satisfied as to the cause of death in all these tragedies ... and I agree with them. None of us sees the bogeymen that seem to be hanging around you and your news-starved reporters. Draper is closing his part of the case and I suggest you do the same. That's all, Chief, you're dismissed."

McKenna angrily turned and bolted out of the judge's office. He needed some time alone to cool off and wash the taste of the judge's condescending tone out of his mouth. Also he had to put together some plan to bring all the unanswered questions to light.

It was now February 2. Chief McKenna was at his desk rereading some of the recent medical examiner's reports, when he received a note from Deputy Draper. The note requested McKenna to come to his office as soon

44

as possible. "Now what?" he puzzled aloud as he reached for his hat and coat.

The walk to Draper's office was short but brisk. The temperature had dipped into the teens, in spite of the welcome sunshine. McKenna's breath turned to billows of white steam as it left his mouth and nose, reminding him there was a lot of winter left. This winter seemed to be a metaphor for the cluster of murder cases he faced. The days were cold, dark and forbidding – as if they hid some unfathomable mystery. He hoped that maybe Draper would shed some light.

"You've been hunting around for a murder, Chief? Well, I guess you finally got one!" The deputy's tone sounded just like Judge Hill's.

"But I don't think it's got anything to do with the Prouty-Hammond case," he added hastily.

"Why don't you let me be the judge of that," McKenna retorted.

"We got a telegram from the sheriff of a little town in Louisiana ... Pass Christian, Louisiana. They found Frank Berry's body by the railroad tracks down there."

It took a few seconds for the words to sink in.

"Frank Berry? The same Frank Berry who worked at Hammond's? The same Frank Berry who lit out of town and disappeared scarcely a week before Henry's death?"

McKenna was out of his chair and staring down at a calm and composed Deputy Draper. The deputy was holding the newspaper as if it were a baseball score sheet.

"How can you sit there and tell me there's no connection?" McKenna said.

"The fact that Berry is dead virtually proves that the killer in this case can strike anyone, anywhere, at anytime!" The chief was livid. "Is everyone deaf *and* blind around here?" He sank back into his chair.

"You want to see the telegram, Chief?"

Draper appeared as though every word had sailed right over his head as he handed the thumb-worn piece of paper across his desk. It was addressed to the chief of police in North Adams, Massachusetts.

"Where has Berry been since he left town? Any clue?"

Draper completely missed the sarcastic barb.

"I don't know about the middle two weeks of January, but he died on Friday, the 20th, and they found him on Saturday."

McKenna nodded and read the telegram:

> *Body of F. X. Berry picked up early Saturday*
> *morning, January 21, on Louisville and Nashville*
> *Railroad here. Stabbed in throat and chest, head*
> *battered, skull smashed. Answer.*
> *Charles H. Tornton, Coroner's Jury*

"Why was it sent to North Adams?" the chief asked.

"It was a mistake," Draper admitted. "The address should have read 'North Adams Street, Spencer.' The telegraph operator must have missed the correct name of the town. I didn't hear about it until a week ago. I've tried to check on it but haven't been able to find out anything ... so I figured I'd turn it over to you."

"Oh, you did?" McKenna resisted the urge to leap over the desk and grab Draper by the throat. "Didn't it occur to you that even the tiniest piece of evidence linking the death of anyone connected to the Hammonds or Proutys could be vital to this ... *my* investigation? You've got a lot of gall to think that any amount of checking on your part would have turned up anything!" Once again, he was letting his frustrations get the best of him.

"Chief, listen, there wasn't a lot anyone could do. Berry was probably in some trouble here in town, which accounts for him leaving so abruptly. Then he probably got into a fight and was thrown off the train ... accounting for his injuries." Even as he spoke the words, Draper sounded more and more uncertain.

"Is that your theory?" McKenna was fuming. "When Berry was thrown from a slow-moving train ... it *was* passing through town ... the tracks somehow reached for him, then rose up and stabbed him in the throat and chest, then coiled around him and crushed his skull? You're an idiot, Draper. Our killer butchered Frank Berry onboard the train, then discreetly dumped his body on the tracks as the train passed through town. And if I don't miss my guess, probably a little after six o'clock in the morning." The chief could feel the connections were beginning to come together.

"What makes you think it was 6:00 a.m., Chief?" Draper asked.

"Draper, if I have my way, you'll be in need of a new line of work in the very near future! Go to the telegraph office, wire the sheriff in Pass Christian, and tell him to send us all the facts he's got on Berry's death. And make sure he sends it to the right town!" He left Draper's office, still angry at the deputy's stupidity.

In less than twenty-four hours, McKenna had men working on every angle of the case. Some were inquiring in North Adams, where the telegram had originally been sent. Other inquiries were made in Boston, and among Berry's friends and relatives in Spencer.

Relatives in town insisted they knew of no reason why he should have left town, nor could they explain how he turned up in Louisiana.

"There is one strange thing, Chief," a cousin of Berry's offered.

"What's that?" McKenna asked.

"A few days before Frank vanished, he told me he needed to make an important trip to Boston. In the same breath, he also said he had an important message to deliver to Henry Hammond. He said he didn't know which of the two tasks was the more difficult. At the time, I thought he was being very cryptic, but this morning it occurred to me that the two events might somehow be connected."

McKenna instantly remembered that Albert Nichols had delivered a message to Henry just a day before he died ... and a few days before Frank disappeared. Nichols completed an errand that Berry wouldn't or couldn't complete, he mused. But what the hell was in the message?

The chief's investigators completed their exhaustive Boston search and found that Berry had been registered at the Crawford House, in Scollay Square, from the sixth to the eighteenth of January. On McKenna's direction, they continued their investigation to establish Berry's movements during that twelve-day period.

Further inquiries made at the telegraph company revealed the original address on the misdirected telegram: "A. Hammond, North Adams Street, Spencer, Mass."

Where did they get Hammond's name? the chief thought. It was now time to head south and get some questions answered.

Two days later McKenna appeared before the town selectmen to ask for expense money for the trip to Louisiana.

"There can be no doubt that Frank Berry was murdered." He began to build his case carefully. "I have received a letter from the coroner's jury in the Berry case. The jury verdict reads ... 'violent death at the hand of person or persons unknown.' "

CRAWFORD HOUSE

CRAWFORD HOUSE,

ON THE EUROPEAN PLAN.

Court St., Corner Brattle St.,

BOSTON, MASS.

STUMCKE & GOODWIN,

PROPRIETORS.

This New and Elegant Hotel, just completed, is now Opened to the Public.
It combines all the comforts of a First Class Hotel at a very
moderate price.

Dining Rooms in Connection,

WHICH ARE THE LARGEST IN NEW ENGLAND. Also an

ELEGANT CAFÉ FOR LADIES.

This Hotel is very central to business, places of amusement, and almost directly at the junction
of *all* the Street Railroads in the City, making it a

DESIRABLE HOME,

For a longer or shorter stay. The prices of rooms will vary according to size or location.

OUR TERMS ARE VERY REASONABLE.

THE DINING ROOMS ARE OPEN ALL NIGHT.

MEALS CAN BE ORDERED AT ANY TIME.

STUMCKE & GOODWIN, Proprietors.

Spencer Town Hall, where selectmen met to discuss the strange happenings.

The panel sat and listened gravely to Chief McKenna's appeal.

"Six upstanding members of this community have died horrible deaths in the last month. As you all know, there is a lot of evil spirit talk in town surrounding the Prouty-Hammond deaths. I'm here to tell you right now that this has been and will continue to be an investigation based on facts. There will be no witch hunts." McKenna's speech began to pick up momentum.

"It might be remotely possible for a wealthy young man, of upright moral character, to willingly die by his own hand, as Henry Hammond allegedly did, or that a frail, sickly woman could strangle herself with a silk scarf knotted around her throat. And it might be possible for four other healthy and prosperous young men to snap emotionally and kill themselves. You all know I don't subscribe to those theories. Nor do I believe Frank Berry's death was a suicide or accident. You must agree that no one is capable of inflicting the kinds of wounds on himself that Frank suffered. I must get to Pass Christian before any and all of the clues to Frank's death are buried along with him. I'm also counting on those clues to shed light on our other so-called suicides."

McKenna felt he'd made a strong case for himself. Now it was time to sit and wait for the panel to deliberate and make its decision.

Minutes passed like hours until finally the door opened and the selectmen filed back in. The chief knew immediately by the looks on their faces that they'd voted him down.

"We're sorry, Chief, but there just isn't any money to throw around on theories and hunches." Selectman Hamelin's grim expression summed up the feeling of the entire panel. "After all, this trip of yours down south could be a wild goose chase."

The chief couldn't believe his ears. But he knew it was pointless to argue once a town ruling was made, especially when money and power wielded such pressure and influence. It was small-town politics as usual. Heaving a sigh of frustration, he knew this was just another roadblock.

A few days later, the Louisiana authorities sent McKenna a property list of items found on Frank Berry's body. It included some very expensive jewelry and a large amount of money. Obviously robbery was not the motive, McKenna thought to himself, feeling somehow vindicated in his original assessment of the crime. Included with the list was a note from the coroner's jury foreman. It was his belief that Berry's murdered body was thrown onto the tracks in a feeble attempt to make it look like an accident. Unless the Pass Christian police could come up with some solid leads, McKenna thought, Frank's murder will go unsolved. He leaned back in his office chair and stared at the ceiling. His conspiracy theory began to look more and more like the truth.

"If this is a conspiracy," he wondered out loud, "it's more far-reaching and all-encompassing than anything I've ever seen ... it's almost as though everyone around here with power and money is in on it. But why? And how do I break through that kind of stone wall?"

Days went by and many of the leads McKenna had been following were getting cold. But early on a Friday morning, things began looking up. One of the chief's oldest friends dropped in for a visit.

Harris Dodge, town treasurer of Charlton, was a burly timberman and lumber dealer, solid and prosperous. The wisps of gossip and rumor surrounding the deaths in Spencer had found their way through the tall trees and rolling New England hills, to Charlton and Harris Dodge in particular.

"Harris! How are you?" the chief greeted his old friend at his office door.

"Just fine, George, and what about you?" They warmly shook each other's hand.

"I've been hearing some interesting stories about some folks who used to live here and what may have happened to them. I thought maybe you could fill me in." Dodge settled into one of the big overstuffed office chairs.

"This has not been one of my better Januarys," McKenna admitted. "There were so many bodies, so many unanswered questions. I tell you it's been overwhelming ..." His voice trailed off.

"Now look, I forgot to offer you some of your favorite police coffee! Just made a fresh pot," said McKenna as he went over to the small stove in the corner of his office and filled two mugs to the brim with the hot steaming brew. "I remember we both like our coffee strong and black."

The chief laughed. God, he thought, it felt good to laugh again.

"Stand a spoon up in it!" Dodge chimed in. "It sure is wonderful to see you again. It's been almost a year."

McKenna recalled a fishing trip the April before.

"Yes, and if I hadn't caught my limit that weekend, we would have starved on that Vermont lake."

They both roared at the recollection. It was but one of the many great memories the two shared over their years of friendship.

They then paused, the room fell silent. Dodge took a deep breathe.

"George, are you still looking into the Prouty-Hammond case?" Dodge leaned forward in his chair.

"I'm afraid that's about all I'm doing. Judge Hill and the rest of his collaborators here in town have virtually blocked all my avenues of investigation. The deputy sheriff and the medical examiner are both involved. I'm certain it's a conspiracy, Harris, but I just can't prove it." He shook his head.

"George, listen to me. I think I may have something that will open this case up for you again." Dodge pulled his chair closer to his friend's desk and lowered his voice. "About twenty years ago, Aaron Hammond did his own selling in the Charlton area. There are people in town today who are prepared to tell you that Hammond was accompanied on many of those trips to Charlton by a woman who wore a veil over her face. The rumors there still surface from time to time. And the identity of his mystery woman has never been uncovered."

"Can't we get any harder evidence than rumors and gossip?" asked McKenna. The chief was positively tantalized by the possibility of a new lead.

"Only one way to find out!" Dodge grabbed McKenna's arm and they both headed for the door.

They proceeded toward Charlton, stopping at every small hamlet, farm and ranch along the way. Some of the older folks in the area remembered Hammond's veiled friend but admitted she never spoke and Hammond never introduced her to anyone. That alone was enough to start the rumors that whirled around the local villages and towns.

"Why would a prominent citizen like Hammond want to be seen with another woman besides his wife. And also, why would she be disguised?" Dodge wondered out loud.

"Part of it must be linked to his wealth and power," the Spencer man offered. "Many folks like that feel as though they're untouchable, that they can do, and get away with, anything. Hammond is no exception ... he figures he can keep *anyone* out of his affairs, including the law. I'm beginning to think he may be right."

After a full day of interviews, the two friends parted company without having gathered any solid new evidence. McKenna's hopes were fading.

When he reached his office that evening, the chief found an unsigned note waiting for him on his desk. The anonymous writer told of a meeting on a back road on the outskirts of town, just two months before Henry's death. Aaron Hammond and Maria Prouty were engaged in a loud argument, but their words were unintelligible. Finally, they parted and went home by separate ways.

Although this didn't actually prove anything, it did lend credibility to some of the wild stories McKenna had been treated to during the day.

The chief decided to see Judge Hill once more. And once more he recounted the facts he'd uncovered concerning Frank Berry's death and the five unexplained deaths in town.

"George, we've been over this ground before! These suicides have been explained to everyone's satisfaction but yours, it seems. Why can't you just let it go ... it's become an obsession with you!" Hill had his fill of McKenna's stalled investigation. "The only murder that was proved was Frank Berry's ... we can't send you to Louisiana ... and you can't solve the case through the mail. Chief, I had asked you to drop this investigation the last time you were in here. Now I'm telling you ... let it go!" With that, the judge stood up as if to leave.

"But I've gone through every angle, talked to dozens of people," McKenna replied as if he were on his last gasp.

Hill relaxed somewhat and sat back down.

"There's no doubt you've done a fine job, George, a very fine job. But this whole thing is out of our hands now. There's nothing more to be done."

Suddenly, the judge switched gears, his expression changing to a broad smile.

"Speaking of good police work, George, I have right here on my desk a recommendation for your appointment to the State Detective Force. The thing for you to do is to accept this appointment ... it's a great opportunity and a significant step up. What do you say?"

Still smiling, Judge Hill leaned back in his chair and knit his fingers behind his head.

"I appreciate the vote of confidence, Your Honor, but with all due respect, I want to stay with the job I already have. I love this town and the people in it ... plus the fact that I can't rest until I've answered the long list of questions I have surrounding these deaths. I'm sorry, sir ... thank you, but I'm sorry." Before the judge could reply, McKenna turned and left.

The hushed whispers that had been skulking around town for the past six weeks now broke into a flood of gossip, rumors and erroneous reports. Half the townsfolk predicted an immediate arrest, the other half a new wave of deaths.

At the following Board of Selectmen's meeting, Deputy Sheriff Draper made a surprise appearance.

"You gentlemen are aware that Spencer and its outlying villages are in great confusion – bordering on hysteria – stemming from the charges and countercharges surrounding the Prouty-Hammond case."

The panel nodded in agreement.

"My assistants and I have investigated each of these cases thoroughly. We are convinced, with the exception of Frank Berry's demise, that the deaths were all suicides and are in no way linked to one another. In Berry's case, the murder took place too far from our jurisdiction for us to investigate promptly and efficiently. You had already decided on this matter when you refused expenses for Chief McKenna to visit the crime scene. I am therefore informing the Board that, as far as my department is concerned, the Prouty-Hammond case is officially closed."

The panel agreed with Draper. The vote was unanimous.

Following the Selectmen's meeting, a town meeting was called. It was convened at the Massasoit Hotel and was presided over by E. Harris Howland, a well-respected member of the community. Many friends of the Prouty and Hammond families, including Dr. Wheeler, were in attendance. A motion was set forth and passed, which compelled both police departments to drop their investigations and finally put the entire matter to rest.

The *Worcester Telegram* reporter, William McDonald, covered the town meeting and decided to drop in on Chief McKenna later that evening.

Having heard McDonald's story, McKenna stood his ground as firmly as ever, explaining, "They can hold all the town meetings and pass all the motions they like, but I'm not letting this go until my questions are answered. I'm not paid to turn my back on unsolved crimes, but I *am* paid to find out who's responsible and prosecute them. I just can't understand why no one else will acknowledge the serious questions I've been posing for the last six weeks. You remember them, don't you, Will?"

McDonald nodded.

McKenna then recalled some of the crime scenes from memory.

"What became of the gun that killed Henry Hammond? And what about the note that Maynard found in Albert Nichols's hand? How could poor, sickly Mrs. Prouty strangle herself? Where is the gun that killed George Dumas? Doesn't it seem to you, Will, that these are legitimate questions requiring honest answers, or am I so obsessed with all this, I lost my perspective on the truth?"

The reporter poured them both a stiff drink.

"Chief, I've been following this case right along with you from the very beginning. There's no question in my mind there is someone with great influence and power behind all this. But conspiracy is very difficult to prove when you're being stonewalled at every turn. If neither of us has answers to your questions, you can't arrest the perpetrator and I can't write what could be the greatest story of my career. I understand your frustration."

McDonald got up, strided across the room and poured them each another drink.

"So what are you going to do?" He looked over at a downcast McKenna.

"I'll keep pushing until something gives."

The chief wished his friend good night and went back to his notes.

The next day, McKenna found himself once again in front of the honorable Judge Hill.

"McKenna, I'm ordering you to drop the Prouty-Hammond case. It's finished, there's nothing more to find out." The jurist pounded his fist on his desk as if it were a gavel.

"What is it, Your Honor? Am I stepping on some important toes?" McKenna asked, his face red with anger.

Hill ignored the remark.

"The state detective job is still open if you want it," the judge reminded him. His voice sounded conciliatory.

"Not interested, Judge," he shot back. "I'm not through with this investigation yet."

McKenna roared out of the judge's chambers, slamming the door behind him as if to punctuate their conversation.

As the six-week investigation plodded on, McKenna had come to count on fewer and fewer supporters. The mood in town had swung over to the sentiments of Judge Hill and his people. But the two local newspapers, the *Worcester Telegram* and the smaller *Spencer Sun*, had stuck it out with the chief. With those newspapers behind him, McKenna knew he could buy some more time.

The following morning the *Spencer Sun* publisher, Elmer Dickerman, appeared at McKenna's office door.

"I guess they've got me, Chief!" the young man blurted.

"What are you talking about, Elmer? Who's got you?" The chief was confused.

"You see, George, I rent my shop from Judge Hill. Well, he threatened to take the property back unless I stop reporting on your investigation into the Prouty-Hammond case. This is a good newspaper, George, and I don't want to throw away all the work I've put into it for the sake of one story." Dickerman was almost in tears.

"He can't do that," McKenna protested. "There has to be some other way around this."

"They've closed off all possible ways of beating them. You know my father is financing me ... well, he's been around to see me, too. He and the judge are in this together, and if I publish one more word, the money will dry up and I'll be out of business. I'm sorry to let you down, George, but I have no choice."

Having given in to powerful influence and pressure, Dickerman left McKenna's office, upset and humiliated. The chief felt his support crumbling around him like the walls of an old building.

Next in line was Eddie Park, crime writer for the *Boston Globe*.

"Well, Chief, I'm pulling out. The whole town seems to be behind Hill and his cronies. Nobody is saying anything. The paper won't let me stay here unless I can come up with a new angle. Can you give me anything?" Park was genuinely interested.

Judge Luther Hill was austere and stubborn -- he didn't speak to his wife for thirty years.

Publisher Elmer E. Dickerson offered a cash reward for information that might solve the case.

"I'm sorry, Eddie, I can't. As much as I want to resolve this, I'm not going to start making things up just to keep you on the story. Thanks for all you've done. I'll contact you if I come up with any new leads."

Park wished his friend McKenna good luck and took the next train back to Boston.

Later that day, Chief McKenna decided it was time to pull all his facts and theories together and compile them into a complete and concise report, a definitive restatement of exactly what had transpired in the last six weeks. Working through the day and most of the night, he finally held in his hand what he believed to be a detailed explanation of the Prouty-Hammond mysteries.

The last twenty-four hours had given McKenna a lot of time to think about what his next step should be.

"Is this long uphill battle with all its setbacks and frustrations really worth it?" he wondered aloud. "It could be that all these dead ends are going to stay dead ... or maybe I've lost my perspective and I'm looking at all this the wrong way."

Once he finished his report, he decided his last official act would be a letter of resignation. Rather than feeling a sense of guilt or defeat, McKenna felt somehow exhilarated and relieved, even unburdened.

He sent the report to Judge Hill along with his resignation. His career as an officer of the law was over, but not the Prouty-Hammond case. There was much more work to be done.

When news of McKenna's resignation reached Will McDonald's ears, he was furious. It seemed the power brokers in Spencer were clamping the lid down on their conspiracy tighter than ever. And now there was no one in authority willing to finish the investigation.

McDonald reported directly to the *Worcester Telegram* publisher and editor, Austin Cristy. Cristy had carefully followed McDonald's accounts of the mysterious deaths in Spencer, so he was prepared when his young reporter came storming into his office.

"I'm going to keep after this thing, Mr. Cristy. We can't let them bury murder evidence and our story along with it! They can't keep us quiet!" the outraged reporter declared.

"Will, settle down," Cristy replied. "I'm behind you all the way! Just tell me what you want to do."

McDonald drew a chair up to the editor's desk. His tall, lanky body appeared straight as an arrow as he sternly announced, "I want to write the whole story as completely as I can. I've got plenty of notes to work from and I can get George McKenna to fill in the blanks. What do you think?"

Cristy was impressed with his reporter's enthusiasm.

"You write it, Will, and I'll publish it!"

They shook hands. Will was now set to get right to work.

McDonald was young but dedicated, and he was a resourceful reporter who left nothing to chance. His exhaustive research led him through hundreds of pages of notes, reprints of his earlier articles, and interviews with all the principals, including Chief McKenna. He put together background histories of anyone and everyone he could find connected in any way to the Hammond family.

Once the enormous work was complete, he decided it was too long a piece for one edition. His readers wouldn't be able to digest that much information at one time. It would be better to make it a series of features that would run between four and six consecutive Sundays. Cristy agreed with this and McDonald began to dissect the piece into manageable segments.

Early the following Monday morning, McDonald met with Cristy and the newspaper's legal advisor, Rufus Dodge. The three spent the next two hours reviewing the manuscript.

"This is quite a story, Will," Dodge admitted. "It could raise a few eyebrows in this part of the state ... maybe more if the national syndicates get a hold of it. Have you thoroughly confirmed all your sources? We could be in for a terrible lawsuit if you're wrong about just one detail." He scrutinized McDonald's face.

"I've checked every fact, every interview and every biography for accuracy, sir. I'm positive it's all there!" Will beamed.

"What do you think, Cristy?" Dodge asked.

"This is one of the best pieces of editorial writing I've ever seen, Rufus," replied Cristy. "Will, it's an excellent piece ... congratulations."

McDonald was beside himself with joy. He hitched up his team of horses and hurried into Spencer to tell McKenna the news.

"Will, this is a great story!" McKenna roared his approval at McDonald's work. "Now maybe you'll breathe some new life into this case ... and make some interested folks sit up and take notice. I can't wait to see their faces!"

The thought that somehow his long investigation might finally bear fruit was positively exhilarating.

"Come along, my young friend, the drinks are on me!" McKenna shouted as the two ambled over to the Cabana Saloon for an evening of celebration.

All the regulars showed up that night, and all were treated to Will McDonald's recent success story. Some were still reticent about opening old wounds and possibly realizing new ones. Others cheered the reporter's ability to set the story straight once and for all.

A week before the first feature was to appear, Cristy summoned McDonald to his office.

"Will, we can't print your feature, I'm sorry." Cristy's pseudo apology was lost on McDonald.

"Can't, or won't?" Will fumed. "You, Rufus and I were all in agreement this was the story of the decade! What happened? They got to you too, didn't they?" he shouted.

"I don't know what you're talking about, Will. And please save your accusations ... you're walking a very thin line!" Cristy scolded.

"You know very well what I'm talking about. This is just another roadblock bought and paid for by the people who can least afford to have this story come to light ... the power brokers in Spencer!"

His body began to shake with anger and frustration.

"You said this was one of the best editorial pieces you'd ever seen! Was that a fabrication?" McDonald was seething.

"No, it wasn't a fabrication, Will. It's a wonderful piece. But the legal department decided there were too many potential trouble spots that could invite major lawsuits against us."

The publisher appeared to choose his words very carefully.

"It's time to put this story to rest ... let it go, Will."

"Where have I heard that before?" McDonald muttered angrily under his breath.

"I'm ordering you to let the story fade away until it no longer exists. If you don't, I'll be forced to let you go." Cristy dismissed McDonald with a wave of his hand.

Will's story died, and along with it any hope of solving the Prouty-Hammond murders. Even the gossip and rumors evaporated for a time until, in early spring, McKenna's friend Harris Dodge was found shot to death, an apparent suicide.

McDonald, in his own way, tried to keep up with the lives of the people who had been connected with the case. After many years, the stories which sprang from the Prouty-Hammond tragedies faded away, and the so-called "evil spirit" was finally exorcised. McKenna's many questions were never fully resolved nor was the notion that a secret evil force was at work. Those who might have answered these questions never spoke about them and went to their graves knowing the truth about what really happened in the first two months of 1899, in Spencer, Massachusetts.

TWO

Randy was right. Was this a conspiracy? Absolutely! And what a travesty of justice! It was an indictment of the entire judicial system. The revulsion Marilyn felt at the mindless atrocities began turning to anger, and with it, a desire to expose the serial killer once and for all.

"Where's Randy?" she whispered to herself. "Of all days to be out doing errands. Hurry home, I can't wait to talk to you!"

Her mind was racing. Where to start first? Would it even be practical to think that she and Randy could come close to resolving any of Chief McKenna's unanswered questions or proving his murder theory? After all it had been ninety-one years since those gruesome deeds had occurred.

When Randy finally came home and saw the look on his wife's face, he knew how she'd spent her afternoon. One look told him she understood what he and her brother had been talking about.

"It's monstrous!" she blurted. "I've never seen or heard anything like it in my life. Maybe if we start digging a little, we can uncover what really happened. Randy, I just feel like this has somehow been given to us to solve. What do you think?" She didn't even try to conceal her excitement.

"You're talking about a tremendous amount of time and expense, Marilyn. And it's very possible we could run into stone walls, the same way McKenna and McDonald did." Randy suddenly found himself playing devil's advocate.

"Oh, come on," she pleaded. "We can do a lot of the leg work ourselves ... we don't need to hire anyone. We've got the time, so what have we got to lose?"

"The money!" he replied with a laugh. "I'm kidding. You're right, as usual. I think we'd better find some answers so I can start sleeping again!"

Randy made a fresh pot of coffee and the two sat down to review the story.

"You know, Randy, I bet Linda and Dave would love to get involved in our investigation ... they're adventurous. And we can use all the help we can get."

"Yeah, but first we've got to convince them to read the story."

Randy rose from his chair, moved over to the sink and rinsed out his cup.

They both awoke the next morning without having slept very well. Fitfull dreams repeatedly drove them back in time to 1899, to relive the horror story again and again.

After a quick breakfast they hurried over to Dave and Linda's house, just a few minutes drive away. After parking the car Randy got out and walked over to the house. He peered in through the office window and spotted Dave sitting at the computer. Dave, sensing Randy's presence, looked up at that moment and waved him in. Marilyn followed.

Upstairs, Linda was staring out the kitchen window watching the sky cloud up again. Six days in a row of terrible weather and no sign of clearing, she thought to herself. She lifted the hot cup of French Roast to her lips. Maybe the coffee would help. Then she thought of how the bad weather was compounding the feeling of depression she felt from the recurrent nightmares and the resulting lack of sleep. It had been a long New England winter, and the arrival of spring had brought chilly, overcast skies and plenty of damp weather. Her quiet reverie was interrupted by her husband's voice over the intercom.

"Honey, can you come downstairs? Randy and Marilyn are here and they have something important to talk to us about."

The intercom clicked off.

"Sure thing, I'll be right there," she answered.

Turning towards the bedroom door, she asked herself out loud, "I wonder if there's anything wrong?"

Linda hurried down the narrow stairway through the family room and into their home office. Randy and Marilyn were standing across from the big oak desk when she entered the room.

"Well, this must be important. You two don't usually show up this early!" Linda teased.

Randy got right to the point.

"We have a favor to ask of both of you. We'd like you to read a short story we brought along with us. In a nutshell, it's about six unsolved murders that took place here in Spencer almost a hundred years ago."

He spoke slowly and very deliberately.

"When you've finished it, we'd like your honest opinions."

It was pretty obvious to Linda and Dave that their friends were held spellbound over the old mystery.

"You act as if you've stumbled onto some deep, dark secret. Have you?" Linda asked.

Marilyn's green eyes squinted as she nervously puffed on her cigarette. Her perfect peaches-and-cream skin tones turned pale as she answered.

"Once you've read the manuscript, you'll have a clearer understanding of what we have here. We want to see if it moves you like it did us." Randy nodded his head in agreement.

Marilyn crushed out her cigarette and then paused for a moment as if organizing her thoughts.

"Have you ever heard of the Prouty-Hammond murders?"

She looked into Linda's eyes and then Dave's.

Linda shot a glance over at her husband who was seated behind his desk. Their eyes locked on each other for a few seconds. Randy shifted his body nervously in the silence.

Marilyn broke in.

"Listen, we've been friends for along time ... talk to us. You've heard of this story, haven't you?"

At this point Linda confessed that she had.

"I never intended to keep anything from either of you. Back in the days when I owned the beauty shop, an old customer of mine, who was a great storyteller, told me a tale which, at that time, I thought to be an old legend. I was enthralled by the romance and intrigue. I thought of researching the story then, but I knew I wouldn't have much free time."

Linda moved over to David's desk.

"That's it?" Randy demanded. "Just an old legend? It seems to me the way the two of you were looking at each other, there'd be a lot more to this." Again, he shifted his weight uncomfortably.

"Please, sit down and let me explain ... okay?" Linda had dramatically softened her tone.

"In July 1970, Dave's folks decided to remodel their bathroom. In order to rough in the sink plumbing, they removed one of the old wall partitions. Hidden inside they found a parcel wrapped in an 1899 edition of the *Worcester Telegram* ... I don't recall which month. Inside was a pistol, and from the looks of it, a very old one. A few years later when I learned about the Prouty-Hammond deaths, the damnedest thing happened. My thoughts suddenly flashed back to the moment Dave's dad showed us the gun he'd found in the wall. I've never been able to figure out why my mind made that connection. It actually scared me, and I tried to forget about it."

Randy and Marilyn sat motionless. Could a possible hundred-year-old clue have just shown up in front of them?

"I'm sorry I didn't mention the story to you." Linda continued. "I just took it for granted that you'd heard it like everyone else in town."

"We just found out a few days ago," Randy said. "Marilyn's brother found this manuscript while he and his partner were cleaning the attic at one of the old Prouty mansions. He was quite shaken when he brought it to us and insisted that we read it. Now we need your input. That's why we came by." He paused a moment. "Doesn't it seem strange that the four of us would find ourselves with this murder mystery *and* a possible murder weapon?"

Silence came over the room as they each considered the implications of Randy's last words. Linda shuddered but was still intrigued enough to want to read the story. Her husband agreed.

Suddenly, Marilyn jumped up.

"Dave, let's see the gun!" She was insistent. "Where is it ... is it here?" She couldn't contain herself.

"Well, I don't know, Marilyn. I'll have to look for it. How would you know what kind of gun was used?" David wasn't prepared for the intensity of her interest in the weapon.

Randy's gold-flecked blue eyes widened with excitement.

"The revolver is described in detail in the story. We'll be able to prove it's the same make ... harder to prove it's the same gun ... but it's a start!"

Without another word, Marilyn handed the manuscript to Linda. She hoped, as her brother did, that some peace of mind would come to her by passing the story on. She was partly right.

"We want you to call us as soon as you've finished reading it," Randy called over his shoulder as he and his wife left. "And look for that gun!"

"We will," Dave assured him.

Dave turned to Linda. He rubbed his hand over her dark shoulder- length hair, and looking into her wide hazel eyes, asked, "Are you ready for one hell of an adventure?"

"I think so," she said quietly as they both embraced.

She loved the security she felt when he held her. His dark good looks excited her as much today as they did when they first met. She was still hopelessly in love with him after twenty years of marriage. She hurried off to a small study nestled in a corner of the family room. With its built-in bookshelves and a small window that sent light-filtering shadows dancing across the floor, it was one of her favorite rooms. All was quiet except for the sound of raindrops pattering against the window.

She curled up in the deep-cushioned sofa. Her heart raced with anticipation as she turned to the first page. Gradually, she lost all sense of her surroundings. She then felt a presence in the room. Her eyes widened with fear. Was it her imagination, or did she hear a faint whisper, or a sigh? She had a strange feeling that someone was guiding her through a maze – someone who wanted to make sure that the story was told, that history was set right, and that the spirits of the slaughtered innocents could finally rest.

A chill came over her as she recalled Randy's earlier question. Had someone actually decided *they* should be the ones to pick up the trail of a one-hundred-year-old serial killer, and be given clues to help them find the truth?

"Oh, God," she whispered to herself as she pulled the Afghan up under her chin.

A little later she walked back into Dave's office and stood across from his desk.

"Dave, I've just finished." Her face was ashen.

"I'd say you look like you've seen a ghost, but then again, you just might have. Here, let me get you some water."

She sank down into a chair.

"Maybe you'd like something a little stronger?" he added.

"No, no, just water," she insisted. "The story reminded me of one of those dreams where I'm free-falling, with no parachute, and I'm trying to scream but nothing comes out."

She sat up a bit, gulped some of the cold water and continued.

"Never in my life have I felt sensations as ominous as the ones I'm feeling now. It's your turn, Dave, this is an unbelievable story. You have to read it!" She hurried over to the desk. "Let me know when you've finished, Dave. I'm calling Marilyn now."

When Marilyn answered, Linda was breathless.

"It's incredible, Marilyn, just incredible. This story has to be researched ... and we've somehow been chosen to do it! We need to sit down and formulate a plan."

"What does Dave think?" Marilyn asked with enthusiasm.

"I don't know, he just started reading. I think he'll be impressed with the plot but will probably dismiss the rest as being a town's overreaction to a series of coincidences. You know Dave, there can never be a shadow of a doubt."

Later that evening, the two couples met again at Dave and Linda's to decide what to do next. Linda, Marilyn and Randy all agreed there was something about the story that had hooked them. Each of them, however, had a different idea of what exactly it was. Dave, ever the skeptic, offered nothing at first. He was deep in thought.

"Dave, we'd really like your input on this," Marilyn asked.

He sat back in his chair, half smiling, half serious. He looked at her and said, "I hope you realize how difficult this is going to be. You're going to ruffle some pretty influential feathers in town. A hundred years may have passed, but those names are still important and respected."

"We can't worry about what other people think," Marilyn stated confidently. "This is something we've got to do!"

Linda and Randy both agreed. Outnumbered, Dave conceded.

"Well, we'll need a plan," Dave said. "We can't go off half-cocked. If we're all determined to do this, let's do it right."

"Before we do anything, let's see the gun," blurted Randy excitedly, wanting to examine the evidence right away.

"Is it here in the house?" he implored Dave.

Dave stood up and moved his chair away from the table.

"After my dad passed away, I moved everything from the McDonald Street house over here ... including the gun. I have it packed away somewhere in the bedroom."

He left the room to search. Randy got up and paced back and forth in the kitchen. Linda and Marilyn waited silently, lost in their own thoughts.

After a few minutes Dave returned. He was carrying a folded American flag.

"This flag was used to cover my dad's casket at his funeral," Dave explained.

He carefully unfolded it, revealing what was inside. No one spoke as he lifted the weapon to show them.

"This is definitely the gun my dad found in the wall of his house."

Still silence. Their eyes widened at what they were witnessing.

"Let's see if we can match it to the description of the gun in the story."

Dave looked up at his three partners.

"Hey, come on, it's just an old revolver that probably wouldn't even fire if it were loaded."

Marilyn and Linda backed away, wanting no part of the awful weapon.

"I can't get over what good condition it's in," Randy remarked. "It looks mint!"

Dave turned it over in his hand and noticed two letters inscribed across the thick part of the handle, just in back of the trigger: "F&W".

"What are the odds of this being the actual murder weapon?" Linda asked, uncomfortably. "I can't believe the story and the gun both show up at the same time. It seems strange, almost eerie."

"Linda, we can't be sure yet," Dave responded.

"Just the sight of that gun makes me terrified." Her voice trembled. "What about the markings 'F&W'? What do they mean?"

"They stand for Forehand & Wadsworth, the company that manufactured the gun," Dave explained.

"Give me one good reason why anyone would hide it inside a wall in your father's house," Linda asked, looking sharply at Dave.

He opened his mouth to speak, but before he could, Linda cut him off, reminding him, "I can still remember your father holding it in his hands. I told you then it was linked to something horrible, and I still believe it's true!" The anxiety in the room was building.

"Linda's right, Dave. This all seems too weird," Marilyn said.

"All right," said Dave in exasperation, "let's all just take it easy. "There's one way to begin our search. I'll call one of my customers in town, a gunsmith, and see what he can tell me about it."

He found some old newspapers and rewrapped the pistol.

"Dave, do you think this is the same weapon that killed Hammond and Dumas?" Linda was insistent.

Before he could answer, Randy broke in.

"Linda, you know Dave won't accept anything unless it's written in stone. First, let's get the gun checked by a professional. We'll look pretty damn silly running around assuming facts that aren't yet evidence. I know we're all excited, but someone has to keep all of this in perspective."

He looked over at Dave and continued.

"I think the only thing we're going to establish from the gunsmith is the year in which it was made. Placing it at the murder scenes and proving it was the murder weapon will be difficult, if not impossible." Linda nodded in agreement.

Randy reached across the dining room table and, for the first time, held the revolver in his hands. He suddenly got very cold, his face turning a pasty white. He became disoriented and lost his balance. Dave and Marilyn reached out to steady him.

"Randy, what is it?" Marilyn asked almost in a state of panic. "Please, get him some water!"

Like his fitful dreams, he felt adrift as another reality took over. The silhouettes of two men appeared, their voices screaming inside his head like the ringing of some enormous church bell. Then a terrific sound, almost like a loud explosion, brought him back to the present.

"Randy, are you all right?" Marilyn asked. She helped him with a sip of water and a cool cloth to his forehead.

"Yeah, I'm okay, but for a moment I felt like I had an out-of-body experience. There were loud voices, then screams."

All four of them were now affected and wondered what lie ahead.

The .32 caliber F & W as it is today.

THREE

At precisely 10:00 a.m., the following morning, Linda met Randy, Marilyn and Marilyn's brother, Bobby, in the parking lot of the Richard Sugden Library.

"Linda, we've got some unexpected help, as you can see," said Marilyn as she took her brother's arm. Linda recognized Bobby immediately.

"It's good to see you again, Bobby. We can sure use your input."

Linda smiled and ushered them through the huge oak doors into the library's main reading room.

The old stone building was steeped in local history and color. It was a superb example of Neo-Federalist architecture, prevalent at the turn of the century. Inside, completely restored mahogany wainscoating graced the high walls.

The well-kept hardwood floors echoed their footsteps as they made their way through the stacks of books to the librarian's desk. They were approaching the point of no return.

Marilyn spoke first.

"Good morning! We're interested in any newspaper accounts you might have on microfilm concerning the Prouty-Hammond deaths in 1899. And if there's anything on paper ... documents, letters ... we'd very much like to see those as well."

The graying librarian looked over the top of her steel-rimmed glasses.

"Why would you want to relive that black chapter in Spencer's history?" she asked.

The question surprised Marilyn. Still, she was quick to respond.

"We're doing a project on the late 1800s. If you would be kind enough to let us view the microfilm, we'd appreciate it very much."

Without a word, the librarian turned to a large chest of drawers near her desk and began searching for the film. She glanced over her shoulder once or twice. It made them feel uncomfortable.

Finally, she turned back to Marilyn and handed her the film.

"Be very careful with this," the librarian muttered. "Return it back to me directly."

Linda and Marilyn looked at each other.

"I guess there's still a lot of interest in the Proutys and Hammonds," Marilyn replied.

They found an unoccupied table and settled in to begin their task. Marilyn was lost in concentration. Where should she begin?

"Linda, did you bring the original story?" she asked.

"Yeah, I did. I made a copy, too. Here's yours."

"Great, we can use it to verify dates. Here's an article dated 1941 ... let's see how closely it compares with our story."

Looking across the large wooden table in the middle of the room, Linda noticed how carefully Marilyn pieced the story together. She prided herself in being thorough.

After a short while, Marilyn asked her husband to bring over the stack of local history books he'd gathered. They sat down and proceeded to scan meticulously each volume for anything that pertained to the story.

Bobby and Linda began their search through the great many spools of microfilm, the day-to-day diary of Spencer at the end of the nineteenth century. When they reached January 1899, the bold italic headline provided them with exactly what they were looking for. Waves of excitement rolled over them. It was undeniably Henry's obituary! The words came alive on the viewing screen, unveiling the ugly reality of what had seemed impossible until now.

"This write-up sounds crazy," Bobby whispered to Linda. "How could people have believed such nonsense! Look what it says ... Henry 'too timid to marry?' Get real!"

TOO TIMID TO MARRY, LAD SHOOTS HIMSELF!

ONLY EXPLANATION FOUND FOR THE SUICIDE OF
HENRY HAMMOND OF SPENCER.
FROM FOND TALK WITH BRIDE AND HOME
PEACE, A QUICK MOVE TO DEATH.
Mirror Is Used To Direct His Aim and All Shows Clear Plan.

Special to The Telegram

SPENCER. Jan. 6—With everything to make life worth living, with no apparent motive in sight, Henry Hammond, only child of Aaron Hammond and wife, shot himself in the forehead at 6 o'clock this morning in the library of the fine residence of his parents, 27 High street.

He was 23 years old. He was engaged to be married Tuesday evening at 6 o'clock to Miss Iris G. Prouty, older daughter of William H. Prouty of the boot and shoe manufacturing concern of Prouty Bros.

Words cannot express the anguish of the bereaved parents of the dead young man. The deep sorrow of the boy's fiancée is pitiful.

Both the Prouty and Hammond families are among the most prominent in Spencer, and scores of friends have expressed sympathy today.

Invitations had been sent out to many friends. The ceremony was to be performed Tuesday evening at 6 o'clock by Rev. Sherman W. Brown at the bride's home, Ash and Cherry streets. The bride's trousseau was ready and the groom had bought his wedding clothes. The ushers selected were Millins W. Prouty and E. Bruce Dunn.

Last evening the young man called on Miss Prouty and they discussed final preparations for their wedding. Young Hammond appeared to be in the happiest of moods. Miss Prouty had a slightly sore throat and Mr. Hammond left early. He gave no indication of having a desperate purpose in his mind.

The young man went home and appeared to be jolly. His mother and a cousin, Miss Florence L. Johnson, had not retired and the three sat up to talk. Henry, before retiring, went into the cellar for apples for his mother and cousin. No allusion was made by the young man as to any motive for unhappiness.

He had everything that makes life worth living and loving, indulgent parents, youth, health, wealth, an assured social position and a fond sweetheart, soon to be his wife.

There are, among his friends, many who say Henry Hammond died by reason of an accident, and not of his own volition.

Henry was stalwart and broad-shouldered. At his father's place of business he was reckoned the strongest man there. He was gentlemanly and generous. He was even-tempered and, apparently, did not have an enemy in the world.

His only failing was his overwhelming bashfulness. He was painfully diffident, and, although one of the sturdiest young fellows in Spencer, he was one of the least assertive. Being an only child, his every wish had been indulged and he grew to manhood more retiring in his nature than most young men.

He seldom took part in social gatherings, and while he was welcomed in the best families in Worcester county and had the entree to every social set in Spencer, he rarely went out. He liked horses and owned a fine team.

Henry was 23 years old, Dec. 19, last, and was born at 596 Main street, Worcester, where his parents lived for years. He attended grammar school in Worcester and six years ago next June came to Spencer with his father and mother. He attended Becker's business college and then took charge as chief clerk at the Aaron Hammond wholesale meat refrigerator, Spencer.

The Hammonds, father and son, were very fond of one another, and it was arranged that Henry and his wife should go to live at the Hammond home on High street. The two men usually cared for their horses in the stable at rear of the house, and this morning, in accordance with the custom, they both went to the stable. After they returned to the house, Henry entered the library and, judging from appearances, made immediate preparations for death. He took a revolver from a drawer in his own desk in the library and carefully removed the chairs and other furniture from his way. There is a lounge in one corner of the room with a diamond-shaped, French-bevel mirror hanging on the wall above it.

Henry stood aside the lounge, facing the glass, and by the mirror, was able to aim the weapon at his head. He held the revolver in his right hand, the barrel pressed against the middle of the forehead aiming slightly downward. Shattering the bone, the bullet deflected downward passing through the bony socket of the left eye, shattering the optic nerve and badly discoloring the flesh. The bullet lodged deeply in the head at the base of the brain. Death was probably instantaneous.

Mr. Hammond, sitting in the kitchen, only a short distance away, heard neither the report of the shot nor the thud of the falling body.

The corpse was discovered by Maggie Johnson, a domestic employed by the Hammonds for 15 years. She went to announce that breakfast was ready and found the body on the floor of the library. Henry lay upon his back with his head lying in a little pool of blood, which had oozed from the gaping hole in his forehead. The left hand was lying across the breast and the right arm was outstretched partially beneath the lounge.

The revolver lay on the carpet between his feet, still smoking when the servant found the body. Only one shot had been fired. A gas jet in the library had been lighted.

Aaron Hammond sent at once for Dr. E. W. Norwood, who is medical examiner for this district. Life was extinct. The doctor gave his verdict as probable suicide and allowed preparations for burial to be made.

The young man left no note or letter to indicate why he should prefer death to life.

Fields M. Prouty, uncle to Henry's betrothed wife, carried to her the news. Accompanied by her cousin, Millins W. Prouty, she was driven to the Hammond house. Miss Prouty is an estimable young lady and her position is keenly felt. Word of the tragedy was sent to W. H. Prouty, the young lady's father who was in Boston, and who reached home this noon.

The weapon with which the deed was committed is an old-fashioned .32 caliber revolver of Wadsworth & Forehands make, made in 1876. Five chambers were loaded and one of these had been discharged. The weapon had not been used for years and had lain in a drawer of Henry's desk in the library, forgotten.

Aaron Hammond, father of the dead young man, is proprietor of the wholesale commission meat refrigerator on Wall street, Spencer, and is accounted one of the wealthiest men in town. He is a distant relative of the Hammonds of Hammond, Indiana, millionaire provision dealers. Levi L. and George H. Hammond are brothers and Mrs. Dwight E. Aldridge is a sister, all of Charlton.

Mr. Hammond was interviewed at his home this morning for The Telegram. In speaking of the tragedy, he said: "My boy was over-sensitive and that is the reason I attribute to be the cause of his self-destruction. I do indeed feel most deeply for that poor young lady. It is sad for my wife and for me.

"Henry was essentially a home boy, always fond of his home. When he was a young boy he had more than the ordinary amount of playthings and evinced more liking to play at home than to go away. He and I always did our own chores.

"This morning I got up first and shook up the fire. While I was attending to the boiler, Henry got up and we went out to the barn. I fed the horses and came in to sit down in the kitchen and wait for breakfast. Henry came in a minute or so later, and sat in a chair close to mine. He got up and as I thought went to the rear of the house, but instead went into the library. The maid said: 'Breakfast is ready, Mr. Hammond,' and I

waited for Henry. The maid called again. Then she took a lamp and pushed open the library door and found him lying there. He was all his mother and I had lived for and we are left desolate now."

Henry had always expressed repugnance at the bare mention of suicide, and lately had a discussion with Albert L. Nichols of East Brookfield, clerk for Aaron Hammond. In the drawer of his desk at the refrigerator, Henry kept a revolver of modern pattern, with a placard warning against danger, as the weapon was loaded.

Arrangements for the funeral were completed this afternoon.

Services will be at the house at 2 o'clock Sunday afternoon. Rev. S. W. Brown will officiate.

HAMMOND'S SUICIDE

His Family Authorize a General Denial of Causes Other Than His Shyness

Not only the immediate members, but the large circle of friends, of both the Hammond and Prouty families of Spencer, feel keenly that many baseless reports are being circulated regarding the motive for the suicide of Henry Hammond. Both Mr. and Mrs. Hammond feel that their grief is intense enough without having it intensified by being constantly obliged to repudiate statements regarding the affair. Neither Mr. nor Mrs. Hammond see any reason for changing in any way their theory concerning Henry's motive. They, as well as many of the friends of Henry Hammond, say that if the general public knew the extreme shyness and diffidence of the young man, which amounted even to a peculiarity, they would cease to wonder at this reason being assigned. It was a great trial for a person of his disposition to enter into society at all, and it was rarely that he did so.

Friends of young Hammond remember that he had said to them that he dreaded going through the ordeal of the ceremony, and did not see how he was ever going to get through it, and his friends firmly believe that this preyed upon his mind until his reason became temporarily affected and he was thus led to take his own life in a moment of despondency. Certainly, any other reports are declared to be entirely without foundation.

LAST SAD RITES

FUNERAL SERVICES OF HENRY HAMMOND
ATTENDED BY HUNDREDS
NOT A CURIOUS BUT A SYMPATHETIC THRONG

The funeral of Henry Hammond, who took his own life last Friday, as told in last week's Leader, occurred Sunday afternoon at the home of his parents, Aaron Hammond and wife of High street.

The spacious home was filled to overflowing by people during the ceremony and many more called to offer sympathy to the affected family, who did not remain for the services.

Rev. S. W. Brown conducted the services and he was assisted by the Universalist church quartet, Miss Florence Muzzy, Mrs. W. H. Hathaway, Wm. Hosking and George D. Muzzy.

Miss Iris Prouty, who was to have become the young man's wife on Tuesday, was present at the services.

There was a profusion of flowers and the deceased held in his hand a cluster of roses, a gift of his affianced.

The bearers were Millins W. Prouty, E. Bruce Dunn, Albert L. Nichols, Chas. E. Dunton, Chas. A. Hobbs, Lewis T. Bemis. The first two named were to have been ushers at the wedding.

The remains were placed in the tomb and later will be taken to Hope cemetery, Worcester, and interred in the family lot.

They continued to search for details on the other victims. All were accounted for, with the exception of Albert Nichols.

They noted that the tabloid had stated Maria Prouty's date of death as being the same day as Henry Hammond's: January 6, 1899, when in fact she had not died until the following day, Saturday, January 7, at 6:00 p.m. Might the author have fabricated that particular part of the story to sensationalize it more? It was hard to believe a mystery so spine-tingling could be covered up to keep the macabre deeds a secret. There seemed to be something pretty devious here.

To Linda it was undoubtedly a step into the unknown. It left her wondering why Henry Hammond's demise a hundred years ago sparked a chain reaction of deaths that would echo into the next century, like dominoes programmed to fall in an intricate, yet controlled, even predetermined pattern. How could the townspeople have believed such lies? Why was Chief McKenna and Will McDonald's theory snuffed out? Did old money, along with a prominent judge, allow someone to get away with unforgivable crimes? Linda's mind was full of questions. And it was all so intriguing. She was experiencing an energy that kept pulling her into wanting more answers about the departed souls.

Suddenly the sound of Randy's and Marilyn's voices interrupted her thoughts. She turned and looked over her shoulder to find them talking with a young lady that was seated near them. Linda could see the woman pointing to the manuscript near Marilyn's hand. What was going on? Randy motioned for both her and Bobby to join them.

Randy stuttered when he introduced them to Eleanor Cole. Linda felt at a loss for words, as an inner voice silently questioned the sudden social situation. Who was this lady, and why would they be speaking with her? At this point she thought it best to be quiet and just listen.

She studied the young woman carefully. Her chin-length, blond hair and crystal blue eyes seemed to spark a memory from Linda's past, but something shadowed it out. Linda knew this woman was linked to the mysterious story. The lady talked easily, her tone of voice almost hypnotic in its effect. Linda, still trying to make sense of what was going on, was unprepared for what was forthcoming.

Eleanor Cole proudly stated that she was the owner of the Prouty mansion at 11 Ash Street, where Maria Prouty died. She referred to it as "Ashcroft." For Linda, meeting the owner of that infamous mansion was an added shock to what was already an unbelievable day.

It seemed odd to Marilyn, with all the books and magazines in the library to choose from, that Eleanor was reading an issue of *Cosmopolitan*. Marilyn asked her if she came to the library often and why she had picked that particular day to come. The blond stranger, who had seemed to appear from nowhere, smiled and replied, "I think it must be fate."

Marilyn thought to herself ... fate?, no way. This was predestined by powers out of our control! Could some strange phenomenon be strong enough for the bodiless voices from the past to lead all of us into a strange situation that would eventually unfold a blanket of truth about the mystery?

Marilyn's thoughts were racing wildly. The sheer coincidence of their being at the library at the same time as Eleanor was perfectly ironic.

Coming back to the reality of the moment, Marilyn remembered a story that was printed on Halloween in the late 1980s. It was about the Prouty-Hammond tragedies – its title, "The Greatest Mystery Ever Told: Spencer's 86-year-old Trail of Tragedy." The journalist wrote a short summary of the story, placing a picture of the Prouty mansion on the front page of the *Feature Parade*. Marilyn remembered that the write-up indicated that the Prouty estate was located on the corner of Cherry and Ash streets. She questioned Eleanor Cole on this.

"There were several Prouty families in Spencer ... some were more affluent then others. The Proutys owned some very fine estates," explained Eleanor.

"We were brought up in this town," Marilyn interrupted, "and with the exception of Linda, we know about its history and how the Prouty name in the 1800s meant Spencer. Even today the Prouty name is held in the highest esteem."

Marilyn turned her attention toward the others and continued.

"Isaac Prouty was the founder of the Prouty Boot Company, a behemoth of a factory complex located right behind this library. William Prouty was a distant cousin to Isaac. The town prospered with Prouty Boot and the wire mills, both providing plenty of jobs."

Eleanor Cole looked surprised.

"Well, you certainly know your town history. However, the mansion on the corner of Ash and Cherry streets was owned by a Thomas Prouty, not William and Maria Prouty. The owners who resided there at the time the picture was taken for *Feature Parade* took it for granted they owned the infamous estate. After all the publicity, I received a call from a town resident who told me that I owned the mansion that held the secrets to Maria Prouty's untimely death. I did a title search of the deed ... I know positively that I own Ashcroft. That's what the Proutys named it – Ashcroft!" With a toss of her head and a faint laugh she added curiously, "And I purchased it on Friday the thirteenth!"

Marilyn and Linda quickly exchanged glances. Before either one could catch their breath, Eleanor Cole gave them her phone number, extending them an invitation to view the estate. Both women quickly accepted, stating they would call and set a time that would be agreeable to all. The young woman hastily stood up and placed her hands on the back of the chair that she had been seated in and pushed it forward so it just touched against the edge of the table. She smiled, turned around and made her way to the main door. The foursome sat there in utter amazement, lost for words.

Dismayed at what had just taken place, the energy Linda had felt earlier was now beginning to diminish. She sat back in a Victorian-style chair next to the library's fireplace. A portrait of Richard Sugden, framed in gold, sat over the mantle, adding a touch of the past. Randy, still trying to grasp what had happened, stood toward the back of the library staring out a window which overlooked the small shopping plaza, the same area that had once been the site of Prouty Boot. Marilyn, only a few feet away holding a history book, dropped one arm free and motioned for the other three to follow her. She needed a cigarette desperately and wanted to go some place where she could talk above a whisper.

They were trying to get their emotions under control as they escaped the solitude of the stately building. Finally, outside in the fresh air, Marilyn could now express aloud her first impressions of what had gone on in the library. She looked back in the direction of the old building and then diverted her gaze to her companions.

"I don't know how the rest of you feel," she said, "but it seemed to me that meeting Eleanor Cole and finding out about Ashcroft was no mere coincidence! It seems our destiny for today has been predetermined." The others remained silent.

It was another link in the chain that had bound them together.

They had put lunch off until 2:30 p.m. Now famished, they hurried over to the small luncheonette on Mechanic Street. Once inside, they grabbed a small corner booth. The foursome were now quiet, mulling over in their minds what had just happened.

Randy broke the silence with nervous laughter, as he went on to explain how Eleanor Cole came to introduce herself to them.

"Marilyn and I were rummaging through some old history books. At one point Marilyn suddenly nudged me. With the hand that was resting in her lap, she pointed to the blond lady sitting at the other end of the table. She was watching us both. Her staring made Marilyn uncomfortable. When the woman summoned up enough courage, she approached us and asked if we were researching the Prouty-Hammond tragedies."

"Can I take your order?" the waitress asked, interrupting their in-depth conversation. She read off the day's luncheon specials.

Anxious to get back to the conversation at hand and being far from calm, Randy pulled out a pack of Marlboros from his shirt pocket. He suddenly seemed unskillful with the cigarette he'd removed from the pack. His hands were trembling as he attempted the motion of lighting it. After several tries he succeeded, inhaling a deep drag, then exhaling with a sigh of contentment. Linda, being a non-smoker, frowned. To her, smoking was nothing more than a disgusting habit. The urge for Randy to calm his nerves, though, was more critical right now than anything Linda might say to him about his incessant smoking.

After finishing lunch they had to deal with the reality of going home and going about their mundane routines. It wasn't easy forgetting about, at least for now, the strange events that had taken place a few hours earlier. They wanted to know more and they hoped to discover the truth about the legendary myth. Before leaving the luncheonette, they agreed to meet at Linda's that evening to follow up with what needed to be accomplished.

Bobby, however, hated to inform them that, at this point, he would have to leave the investigation. He was starting a new job that would require him to be out of town most of the time. He had no choice in the matter – he needed the work. He would keep in touch, though, to see how they were progressing, hoping they could get some answers.

FOUR

Dave greeted Linda as she arrived at the door of their Spencer home. One look at her and he instinctively knew she had found some interesting information. She didn't know where to begin. Removing her over-the-shoulder style brief case, she showed him the paperwork she had already accumulated on the Prouty-Hammond tragedies.

"It looks like you've done your homework!" Dave said with genuine interest. Her eyes widened with excitement as she began to tell him about the chance encounter at the library.

After listening for a few minutes to what his wife was trying to tell him, Dave suddenly blurted out proudly, "I've been doing some homework myself. Around noon today I managed to steal an hour away from the office. I took the gun over to Mark's and he confirmed what we suspected. The gun was manufactured between the years of 1872–1890, in Worcester, Massachusetts, by the Forehand and Wadsworth company! That proves that the gun existed at the time of Hammond's and Dumas's deaths."

But she didn't require proof about the gun. She always knew from the moment she first laid eyes on it that it was connected to evil. And now she knew what the evil was. Still, her husband's verification of the gun's manufacturer was alarming. The realization of having the terrible weapon in their possession made her feel like she was concealing some lurid instrument of death.

Things had been strange enough and now this made it more real. Certainly these peculiar occurrences in her otherwise normal life were no mere coincidences! She was finding it a bit macabre. How could four people from the present be drawn into a century gone by?

Around 7:00 p.m., Randy and Marilyn arrived at Linda and Dave's. After a brief exchange of pleasantries, the two couples sat down in their usual chairs around the dining room table. While sipping his coffee, Dave conveyed the information he had concerning the revolver. Unbeknown to them at this time, however, they were about to be led into more unexplainable happenings over which they would have no control. They knew their next step would be to locate the final resting places of the main characters in the story.

"May I make a suggestion?" Dave asked.

"Go right ahead," Marilyn replied.

"Why don't you contact Ernie Roberts? He's the town historian, a trustee at both the library and Pine Grove Cemetery. I'm sure he would be willing to speak with you."

"That's a great idea," Marilyn said, as she nervously tapped her fingers on the table.

Linda nodded in agreement, then asked her husband, "Could you call him for us? You know Ernie better than we do."

Dave, with his arms folded tightly across his chest, was standing next to Randy. With a nervous laugh he answered, "How did I know you'd asked me that?" Linda pretended to ignore his remark.

A few minutes later Dave made the call. Mr. Roberts was cordial. He said he would be happy to accommodate the ladies. However, he was not sure if he could tell them any further information about the story beyond that which had already been printed.

Thursday afternoon, while Linda and Marilyn interviewed Mr. Roberts, Randy and Dave drove to the court house in Worcester, hoping to learn who, in 1899, was the owner of the McDonald street house. They also wanted to confirm if Eleanor Cole did indeed own Maria Prouty's beloved Ashcroft estate.

That same Thursday, in Spencer, Marilyn and Linda began their journey up High Street. Marilyn pointed out the mansion where Judge Hill had once lived. At the crest of the hill still standing was one of the Prouty twin mansions. The other mansion bought by Aaron Hammond no longer existed. It had been torn down in 1919.

Marilyn lifted her foot off the accelerator, slowing the car almost to a stop. Images of Henry and Iris haunted her. She imagined them as young lovers. It was all so clear, their evening carriage rides together, and then their arrival back at the Hammond estate. She could visualize Henry, gently pulling back on the horse's reins, bringing the beautiful dapple gray steed from his prancing trot down to a walk and finally a stop. She could hear the melodious jingle of the beautiful brass bells on the horse's harness as the animal occasionally pawed the ground and snorted.

Bewildered by the quick onset of the vision that had unfolded, it was suddenly erased and in its place, a frightening scene. She was focusing on the grandfather clock that stood in the elegant foyer of the Hammond mansion. It was chiming out the strokes of 6:00 a.m. Before her was the body of Henry Hammond lying on the floor, a bullet wound in his forehead.

Standing next to the body was a man. Although she couldn't see his face, she knew he had a gun clenched in his hand.

"Marilyn! Marilyn!" shouted Linda.

Shaking her head with a look of confusion, Marilyn realized she must have been daydreaming.

"What's the matter?" asked Linda. "Don't you see the car behind us? He blew his horn twice! What's wrong with you?"

Marilyn couldn't understand why she was being possessed with visions from an unknown past. She was entranced by the revelations coming from the beyond.

"My blood runs cold when I think of what took place on the grounds across the street, a place that no longer exists."

Marilyn's words produced a chilling effect. Linda shook her head as if to get the sound of them out of her mind.

Only a few houses up, on the opposite side of the street, was the Roberts home. Mr. Roberts greeted the two anxious ladies at the side door. He was always a pleasant man, well loved by many in town.

He led them down to his quaint little office in the basement. It contained a desk and a few chairs. His nostalgia for the town was evident in the nineteenth-century vintage pictures and maps hanging side by side on the walls. They were mounted in chronological order and were very well preserved. All this added to the viewer's enjoyment.

Both women took turns asking him questions. With his permission they recorded the conversation for future reference. From memory he related the story article to them, proudly pulling out his copy from a desk drawer. The historian recited what they already knew.

"So sad ..." he exclaimed. "The poor boy took his own life."

This referred to Henry Hammond, they presumed.

When they asked about Albert Nichols, Mr. Roberts raised his head, his eyes widened, stuttering as he began. "The ... the girls ... I telephoned them in Florida when the detailed accounts of the Prouty-Hammond tragedies appeared in that 1941 article. I assured them, they should feel no shame or embarrassment."

Both women were puzzled, speculating on what he meant exactly by that comment. They pondered on what kind of shame or embarrassment could be caused by the publication of such a sensationalized story.

"Albert Nichols was my wife's grandfather, " he revealed.

This came as a total surprise to both Marilyn and Linda. The girls, as he referred to, must be Albert Nichols grand-daughters, they thought. They could see that his recalling the anguish of Nichols's death had taken an effect on him. They decided it was best not to press him about the statement he had made.

Notions began running through Linda's mind. Did Albert Nichols, Henry's loyal friend, know more about the Hammond suicide than he had admitted to? After all, he was the bearer of the mysterious message from Aaron.

Mr. Roberts continued to tell them more about Nichols's private life.

"Just before Albert died, he was a very ill man, both physically and mentally. He was an amateur photographer." Roberts showed them a self-portrait which Nichols had taken in front of the trolley stop in East Brookfield.

Although Linda and Marilyn said nothing, they were overcome with excitement. Finally they had a face to go along with the name.

"He was an unusually jolly-natured person, always telling a joke to everyone he met. We will never know what, in 1902, changed his love for life and family and turned him down the road to self-destruction."

With that Roberts let out a deep breath.

The year 1902 rang an alarm bell in Linda's head. The story had reported that Nichols had died in January 1899, the same month in which the other deaths had occurred. She wondered if it were possible that the writer didn't have all the facts.

"Mr. Roberts, is Albert Nichols buried in Spencer?" Marilyn asked.

"No, no, he was an East Brookfield lad. He's in Evergreen Cemetery."

This was the information they needed. Now they would be able to ascertain Nichols's actual date of death and secure his obituary.

Linda asked if he could tell them where Maria Prouty and her daughter, Iris, were buried.

"Maria was laid to rest in Pine Grove Cemetery. Her grave is way in the back near the fence, I can't quite remember the exact spot. I think Iris is buried in Connecticut but I don't know the name of the town. She married later in life, to a gentleman named Wesley O'Leary."

Mr. Roberts informed them that another person, an author from New York, had tried to obtain some facts about the New England mystery.

"He never succeeded in doing so. He ran an ad in the *Worcester Telegram & Gazette*," explained Mr. Roberts.

He produced the ad from his desk drawer and showed it to them.

Author Seeks Information

March 12,1978

E. Warren Smith, a Brooklyn, N.Y. writer, sends this query:
"For a study of New England unsolved mysteries, I am
seeking any available information or material (photos,
press clippings, personal reminiscences) regarding the
Prouty-Hammond deaths, and related deaths, that occurred
at Spencer, Mass. in January, 1899. These events were
covered by the late William McDonald, a reporter for the
Telegram. All material will be carefully copied and returned."
His address is 169 Columbia Heights, Brooklyn, N.Y. 11201.

Both Marilyn and Linda knew they had their hands on a good story. Many people had tried to get information on the strange mystery but were unsuccessful.

They viewed several old town maps that Mr. Roberts pulled from his collection. Marilyn had a hard time containing her excitement as she tried to point out to Linda, without it being obvious to Mr. Roberts, that a certain portion of Adams Street in the 1800s was the same location where Dave's family home had been built. It was listed as North Adams Street. The map was dated 1884. This was an important discovery for them. The first hint about how the gun might have been brought to the house had just been given to them.

Time had passed quickly and they had stayed longer than they'd planned. Mr. Roberts appeared to be getting tired. They figured it was best to extend him their gratitude and depart since they were genuinely impatient to discuss in privacy their findings on Nichols's death and the North Adams Street location. Next would be a quick stop at the library to obtain Nichols's obituary. Then they would head to Evergreen Cemetery in East Brookfield.

Now it seemed that, at every step of the way, they were being driven by an unknown force. They were picking up small pieces of knowledge from the past which committed them further into the depths of the haunting mystery.

ALBERT L. NICHOLS TAKES HIS

OWN LIFE WHEN VISITING

PARENTS AT

E. BROOKFIELD

Albert L. Nichols, bookkeeper at Aaron Hammond's cold storage house, Wall street, killed himself Thursday evening at his parents home in East Brookfield, by cutting his throat with a razor. Nothing could have been more surprising, except to a few intimate friends and relatives, than this act of Mr. Nichols. His relatives and close associates knew for some time that he was affected periodically with grievous attacks of melancholia. This was owing in large part to the condition of his health. During the summertime he was seriously affected with hay fever which weakened his general system and last summer while in this condition he was vaccinated. The vaccination seemed to have a serious effect upon his general health and he was confined to the house for some time with an illness which followed the introduction of the vaccine virus. It is understood that the physicians maintain that vaccination was in no way responsible for the change in Mr. Nichols' health, but friends say that he has never been the same man since. For the past six months he has not been strong. Three weeks ago he was unable to come to his work at the Hammond refrigerator and sent word one Thursday morning that he was ill. He remained in bed for four of five days and thinking that he might find more quiet and rest at his parents home in East Brookfield, his friends induced him to go there, his family remaining at the home on High street, Spencer. He consented to go for a few days and remained in bed there.

Indications of serious mental and nervous trouble began to show themselves and the condition of his health seemed to prey upon his mind continually, and frequently he would be found crying.

His home relations were extraordinarily happy and he took much comfort and pride in his family of wife and five children.

It was about 6 o'clock Thursday evening that Mr. Nichols' mother heard a body fall in the conservatory off the dinning room. She hurried to the spot and found her son lying face downward on the floor, the blood flowing from a long gash in his throat.

Dr. W. F. Hayward was called in a very few minutes and found the windpipe and jugular vein severed. Medical examiner Norwood viewed the remains an hour afterward. The unfortunate man used his brothers' razor, which was contained in a bureau drawer and standing in front of a mirror committed the act.

For fifteen years he had been employed by Mr. Hammond, just in the East Brookfield refrigerator and later at Spencer when the plant was established here. He was thirty four years old, son of Leroy Nichols, a respected citizen of East Brookfield. Eleven years ago he was married to Miss Hattie Prescott of East Brookfield. They have five children.

A mother, father, and five brothers survive, Dr. Nelson Nichols of Maine, Leon Nichols of Boston, Ralph, Walter and Bob of East Brookfield, and a sister also Mrs. Dufton. Mr. Nichols of late frequently spoke to intimate associates about his friend the late Henry Hammond, with whom Nichols worked at the refrigerator and who took his own life a few years ago. At such times he would cry and appear to be greatly dejected. Mr. Nichols was adept at photography and took great comfort and pleasure in the work. Until within the past few months he was of unusually jolly nature. One of the places which he frequently visited was the Leader office, and always made a tour of the company room with a joke for every employee. Mr. Hammond his employer, placed the utmost confidence in him and the management of the Spencer plant largely devolved upon him.

His afflicted family has the deepest sympathy of everybody. The funeral will take place Sunday afternoon at 3:30 o'clock at his parents residence at East Brookfield. Burial will be at Evergreen Cemetery, East Brookfield.

Albert Nichols headstone.

FIVE

The story was correct about a few things. Nichols did die of a slashed throat and it did occur at his parents' residence. Interestingly, like the others, he also died at the fatal hour of 6:00 a.m. The date of death on his tombstone confirmed the obituary.

Linda felt very uncomfortable standing at his grave, searching for answers that were buried with the victim. She was also uneasy with the strange atmosphere enveloping them. And all this rain to go along with these strange feelings! This was the second time they had ventured into the cemetery when the sky had opened and poured its fury to earth. It had made it almost impossible to search for the old gravestones on which were inscribed the dates that were so important to them. It seemed as if they were being warned by a spirit stronger than the one that had plunged them into the investigation.

Suddenly, seemingly out of nowhere, crows began circling overhead. Their blackness seemed to shadow the large pines bending in the breeze. Linda was apprehensive and wondered if their presence could simply be coincidence or an indication of something else, something which might be warning her of the ominous content of the moment. Digging the heel of her shoe into the wet soil, her eyes cast downward staring at the crevice she had just made in the grass, she said in a low, demanding voice, "I've had enough of this. I want to leave."

During the ride home Marilyn wanted to say something to console her friend. But first she needed a smoke. With her left hand gripping the steering wheel she frantically searched for her cigarettes. Using her free hand she reached inside her black leather bag which was wedged between the two front seats. While trying to keep her eyes on the road, she glanced down, and with a few quick motions, pulled and tugged until finally her hand gripped the small pack of Marlboros. Retrieving a cigarette from the pack, she lit it and began to compose her thoughts.

The words of consolation she sought were not forthcoming. Instead a completely different train of thought entered her mind. Then, in an almost uncontrollable manner, she blurted out, "Look, Linda, you can't let these erratic episodes affect your investigation of this story."

Biting her lip, Marilyn couldn't believe this was all she could say at a time like this. God, I need some help here, she thought to herself.

Linda shifted her body uncomfortably. Turning her attention away from the scenery along Route 9, she looked over at Marilyn and poured out her emotions.

"I can't help thinking that maybe the old reports about the case are true. If you read all of them, you'll find that all the people involved either committed suicide or met with fatal accidents, except for McKenna. We're just at the beginning stages of our inquiry, and already things have become totally bizarre! This is all I think about lately. And look what's happening to Randy! Why is he experiencing such terrible dreams?"

"I don't know," Marilyn replied as she continued puffing on her cigarette, staring straight ahead, concentrating on the traffic. She was a cautious driver and, with the rain getting heavier and interfering with visibility, she was trying to avoid having an accident.

As the great sheets of rain came down Linda became increasingly more possessed by her feelings. Now it was time for her to let Marilyn in on everything that was on her mind.

"You know," Linda said with trepidation, "I've never believed in ghosts or in any kind of apparitions, but I really feel as if I'm being tested by something or someone from the past ... in fact, I think we all are! Frankly, I'm damn scared. Still, I can't stop wanting more answers. I believe there's a dark secret to this story, a secret more disturbing than we could possibly imagine. It's so strange."

Linda stopped for a moment to collect her thoughts and then continued.

"As far back as I care to remember, I've had dreams of living in Victorian times. In those dreams I would see this beautiful mansion set atop a hill. The front lawn was covered with flower gardens which cascaded down to a dirt road, joining a driveway entrance guarded by statues of lions and black wrought-iron gates. I would find myself on this old carriage road looking up at the grand estate, knowing I belonged there. I know it sounds odd, but I believe a series of events in my life has led me here to New England, to this particular town. Think about it, Marilyn. The discovery of the gun hidden in my in-laws' home. The visit with Ernie Roberts and the old maps he let us view, proving our theory about that house, the same place Berry's body was sent. I don't know, maybe I'm making too much of it. But I keep asking myself ... what are the odds of this happening? The story is like a puzzle and I can't help but feel we are the missing pieces."

Before Marilyn had a chance to respond, Linda asked her, "Do you believe in reincarnation?"

As if suddenly, the driveway appeared dead ahead. Marilyn realized that she had lost track of time while listening to Linda's slant on all the recent events. As they pulled in she hit the brakes hard, making the car rock forward, thrusting their bodies in a back-and-forth motion. Marilyn realized what Linda was actually implying.

"Your dream fits the description of the Prouty estate, except for the part about the wrought-iron gates. But who knows ... maybe in the 1800s the gates existed."

"Do you think there is some association with the two?" asked Linda.

"Yes, I think so," replied Marilyn.

Marilyn knew there was an association and now they needed to find it. Reincarnation was a strong possibility. The thought had crossed her mind more than once. She felt the answers for Linda lay within her dreams. Their conversation was interrupted when Randy and Dave pulled into the driveway and parked the Lincoln alongside them. Both women scrambled out of the car, hurrying to question the two men about their findings at the court house.

"Let's go inside where we can talk," Randy told them as he walked toward the front door, his head bowed trying to protect his eyes from the rain.

Once inside, away from the drenching downpour, Linda made a fresh pot of coffee. The foursome gathered in the dining room as usual.

Randy gave a descriptive account of what they had discovered at the court house. Dave was helping him fill in the details of how their pursuit led them through the building, down to the bottom floor, which could only be described as musty, and finally locating the recorded deeds that would supply the information they needed. Marilyn and Linda listened with intensity, hanging on to every word.

Randy confirmed that Eleanor Cole was, without a doubt, the owner of the infamous mansion that Maria Prouty once called her own, the place that held the secrets to the events leading up to her untimely death.

"Dave, tell them who owned your parents' house in the 1800s!" said Randy. Untamed excitement was showing in his bristled blue eyes.

With his eyes fixed on his wife Dave replied, "Adams owned the house. He also owned all the land around the area."

Marilyn broke in, revealing to Linda, "Linda, remember the old maps we saw at Mr. Roberts's house? It all makes sense now ... Adams Street! If you check your Spencer town history, you'll find that Adams used to employ field hands, and they lived on his property."

With more research the two couples would soon learn that Berry had once been a border at the Adams Street address. Some of his relatives worked for Adams.

Marilyn continued. "Dave, I'm calling my mother. I want to ask her if she knows anything about the previous owners of your family's home." Marilyn's parents owned the house next door. It had been in the family for generations.

Dave agreed. Reaching on top of the kitchen counter he handed her the portable phone.

She wasted no time getting to the point. Her mother informed her that the house had once belonged to a cousin of her grandmother Beaudin's, Frank Lariviere.

"Do you still have the piece of petrified wood that your Grandma Beaudin passed on to you?"

"Yes, but what's that got to do with anything? I use it for a bookend," Marilyn replied.

"The painting on that wood is a picture of the Boutillette house as it appeared in the late 1800s," her mother explained. "On the back side is the signature of Mrs. Frank Lariviere, the cousin who did the painting."

"Are you sure it's the Boutillette house?" Marilyn asked.

Her mother was adamant about it.

"Back in those days the front door of the house faced what was known as North Adams Street. It wasn't until some years later, until after they remodeled the house, that the front entrance was placed facing McDonald Street."

Marilyn had her mother's curiosity peaked. She wanted to know the reasons for all daughter's questions. Marilyn told her about the Prouty-Hammond mystery, about the gun, how the four of them found the whole thing fascinating, and how they were trying to research the story to find out the truth.

Her mother's reply came as a surprise.

"I remember the day Phil found the gun and called us over to take a look at it. We thought it was odd that someone would go through so much trouble to hide it behind a wall."

Now Marilyn was indeed convinced they were being drawn into the whole affair by some mystifying force over which they had no control.

SIX

With this startling new revelation, they had now found another link in the chain into the unknown.

It was time for Linda and Marilyn to approach Eleanor Cole and take her up on her offer to let them view the Prouty mansion. Trying to restrain her excitement, Linda contacted Eleanor and made the arrangements. They were scheduled to meet on Monday, the following week, at 4:30 p.m. Linda had hopes of bringing Randy and Dave along, but Eleanor made it clear that only she and Marilyn were invited. Both men were disappointed with Eleanor's stipulation. Randy believed Maria's spirit was dwelling within the mansion, and if he could get inside, he would feel her presence. He knew her spirit was always near them, guiding them along the right path.

The next few days were full of anticipation for all of them. Each was beginning to form his and her own image of what the estate would look like inside. For Linda, thoughts of Maria Prouty's final days at Ashcroft were already beginning to form in her mind. She couldn't help wondering what clues to Maria's death, if any, they would get from walking through the place. Both Linda and Randy had the same feelings about Maria. Somehow her ghostly entity was infusing itself within their earthly souls, affecting them beyond words.

Two nights prior to their scheduled visit, Linda's nightmare came back to haunt her. Finally, after all this time, she realized who the woman was that visited her in her dreams, guiding her to a mansion where she would wander aimlessly. She found herself standing in the parlor of the old estate, staring at her reflection through the mirrored, mahogany mantel of the fireplace. A crackling wood fire was blazing from the hearth below, but it gave no warmth. Only coldness surrounded Linda as the image of Maria Prouty took her by the hand and guided her back to the past, showing her the terrible truth, letting her see and hear a detailed account of that fateful evening. With fear in her eyes and with blood-curdling screams, Maria made a desperate attempt to escape her killer. She ran down the winding staircase, through the hallway, toward the front entrance. Out of the dark a man grabbed her from behind, reaching for her throat. Linda couldn't get a clear look at him but she was sure it was William. He knocked Maria to the floor and pressed his knee against her back, holding her down. She clawed the floor like a dying animal. As frail as she appeared, she still managed to escape his powerful hold but not for long. He ripped her nightgown down over her shoulders. Her long dark hair was hanging in tangled strands, and her lips were covered in blood.

Linda woke up in a cold sweat, breathing hard and quick, frightened as if she, herself, had been the victim. She felt confused. Her mind was racing with questions. Why did the dreams seem so real, so intense? She wondered if the truth about Maria could be coming through her dreams. With her arms down by her side, she pushed herself up and lifted her head off the pillow. She peered at the white porcelain alarm clock sitting on the marble end table.

It was only 4:30 a.m. – she had hoped it was much later. She slumped back on the bed, casually turning her head to look over at her husband lying in a sound sleep. She couldn't bring herself to wake him. She had put him through this too many times. She took a deep breath, trying to calm herself as she lay there motionless, still not believing how detailed the dream had been. She had to get up. Her mind was roaming aimlessly. She was too restless to stay in bed any longer.

She made it to the kitchen, and while pacing back and forth, she kept going over and over in her mind what she had envisioned. For Linda it was becoming a little too bizarre.

Later that morning, Marilyn had some errands to do downtown. Without realizing it she found herself driving down Ash Street. As she neared the former Prouty estate she brought the station wagon to a full stop, just far enough away not to look obvious.

Her eyes fixed on the pale, pink-colored mansion situated atop the hill. She was drawn into the depths of its structure, her thoughts floating, succumbing to a vision of an eighteenth-century bridal gown glistening with pearls and lace, hanging aimlessly in a time past. The exquisite dress was bodiless. The power of Henry and Iris's undying love seemed to reach into Marilyn's soul, screaming out to her, allowing her to see things and hear secrets that no one else could. Marilyn was bewildered by the experience. The visions of so long ago were coming much too often. Never in her life had she dealt with such peculiarities. The next thing she knew she was staring at her back door, not remembering the ride home.

"What was happening?" she asked herself out loud. Her keys were cradled in the palm of her hand. The ringing of the kitchen phone caused her to hurry and fumble as she tried opening the door. Rushing inside she picked up the receiver on the fourth ring. It was Linda.

"Marilyn, where have you been?"

Marilyn could tell by the tone in Linda's voice that she was upset about something.

Without giving her a chance to answer, Linda blurted out, "The nightmares I told you about ... I know what they mean now! A few days ago I couldn't understand the reason or the meaning behind them, but now they're beginning to make sense. The woman in my nightmares is Maria Prouty!"

Marilyn was silent. Her knees felt like rubber. She leaned her body against the kitchen wall to keep from falling. She didn't dare tell Linda what she had experienced earlier.

Both of them were having second thoughts about the abnormal encounters which were leading them into the unknown. Still, they had to press on – their research was far from over. The need to know the truth of Maria Prouty's and Henry Hammond's deaths was more powerful than anything their fears could induce. Marilyn tried to reassure Linda that there was a reason for everything that was occurring. In time she was sure they would have the answers. Right now Linda needed to get herself together. They had plenty to accomplish before they were finished with their quest.

Plans were made for the following day to visit Pine Grove Cemetery on the north side of town. Both women felt it was necessary to locate the grave sites of Maria Prouty and the other related characters involved in their story. They weren't quite certain why, but it seemed the spirits of the deceased were casting them in that direction. Trying to keep low profiles, both women felt it would be better to avoid asking questions at the cemetery office – they didn't want to draw attention to what they were doing. And it really wasn't necessary to ask for the Prouty plot's location because Mr. Roberts had given them a detailed description of where to find it.

The wind picked up as they neared the cemetery entrance. Linda's eyes were drawn to the Prouty name engraved on the bronze plaque which was embedded snugly against the pillar that held the iron gates to the stone wall. Marilyn hadn't noticed it – she was too busy concentrating on maneuvering the large blue station wagon through the narrow opening. A cove of whispering pines shaded the small winding road that led to the main part of the cemetery.

Once inside Linda said, "If people knew we were searching cemeteries, they'd think we were weird! Of course this whole thing is crazy! Just look at us! We're living our lives through this story!"

"You sound just like Randy!" Marilyn replied. "He says the same thing. You both should realize we have to do whatever it takes! There is a reason why we've ended up here ... I believe it's destiny. And it's our obligation to bring this story to the public."

"Marilyn, stop the car ... look!" Linda saw it. Towards the back of the cemetery, near the fence, lay the Prouty family plot, just as Mr. Roberts had described it.

Even though it was only early autumn, it felt more like midwinter. A light snow, mixed with rain, began dusting the leaves that were scattered on the ground. The obelisk-shaped monument's tapered shaft reached toward the sky, making it clearly visible from a distance.

The two women hurriedly opened the car doors and began their trek. As the two ventured closer to the gravesite, they noticed something unusual. Neatly arranged on Maria's headstone were several sea shells, a small pumpkin, and a piece of quartz crystal.

Linda felt the fear rise from the pit of her stomach. With a quick motion she turned toward her friend and asked, "What is the meaning behind this?"

"Yeah, it has me wondering, too," replied Marilyn. "It's as if someone wants to scare us off because he or she knows what we want! It's not going to happen ... we've come too far. Remember, Linda, they're just spirits ... they've done us no harm up to now."

"Well, I don't think spirits are putting the mysterious articles on Maria's headstone. What's your answer to that?" Linda nervously questioned.

"I don't have an answer for it right now, Linda. With a little patience I'm sure we'll come up with a logical explanation."

The wind was gusting with more intensity now. Without saying a word to each other they hurried back to the car. Marilyn inserted the key in the ignition and turned – the motor turned once and then stalled.

"What's wrong?" said Linda nervously.

"I don't know," answered Marilyn.

"Pump the gas pedal," urged Linda.

"I don't want to flood it," said Marilyn with a tone of exasperation.

Prouty Family Stone

Maria Prouty headstone with articles placed on it.

They felt terribly frightened. Linda's eyes grew wide as Marilyn made another attempt to get the motor started. After what seemed like an eternity it finally turned over.

Randy and Marilyn were returning home from a very pleasant weekend getaway in New Hampshire. They had needed a few days of peace and quiet to put some distance between them and all the strange events happening in Spencer.

During the ride back Marilyn turned on the radio and listened to her favorite oldies station, 103.0 FM – "Stranger On The Shore" was playing. She leaned her head back and puffed away on a cigarette, her daydreaming turning to questions about the deaths of Henry Hammond and Maria Prouty. Her thoughts cast a dark veil over her rational intellect, sparking an idea that made it necessary to stop at Worcester's Hope Cemetery to search for the Hammond plot. She knew it wasn't anything out of the ordinary for them to go searching for gravestones.

She soon realized that the next exit off Route 290 would take them right past the cemetery. Before she could tell Randy what she had in mind, a flock of crows swooped down and began circling the car, blinding their view of the road. Randy's knuckles were white from gripping the steering wheel so tightly. He quickly veered from the center lane of the expressway over to the breakdown lane. Marilyn covered her eyes when Randy, now seemingly uncoordinated, almost lost control of the car and just missed the guard rail. He managed to steer the station wagon safely back into the breakdown lane and brought the car to an abrupt stop. His hands still shaking and his knees knocking, he reached across the front seat to console his wife.

"Are you all right?" he asked.

Marilyn drew in a deep breath and screamed at him.

"What the hell is happening? ... this is getting crazy!"

Finally gathering their sanity they cautiously looked around before stepping outside the car. Observing the traffic, it appeared that no other motorists were affected by the erratic behavior of the crows. This was no surprise to them – the birds had fled as quickly as they appeared.

They couldn't help feeling frightened at what had just taken place. It was like a nightmare, only for them it was real. Staring into each other's eyes, looking to one another for answers that would not come, they got back in the car and cautiously drove away, afraid it might happen again.

After they had gotten a few miles down the expressway, Marilyn began to speak to Randy in a more rational tone.

"Before that frightening incident with the crows, I was about to ask you if we could stop at Hope Cemetery to look for Henry Hammond's grave."

"Yeah, why not?" Randy answered. "Who knows what the hell we'll encounter there. Our lives have been turned upside down by this damned crazy story. You know, Marilyn, for the life of me I don't know why I'm still so intrigued with it ... I can't give up on it!"

Marilyn shook her head, agreeing with her husband.

"I know just how you feel," she replied.

Clearing his throat, and with a bit of uncertainty in his voice, Randy said, "I've been getting this feeling ... it's like a message that keeps playing over and over in my head ... like someone is trying to communicate with me. I can't explain it. In the last few weeks I've had a feeling that I'm going to find something along the side of the road. I don't know what it is."

"I hope it's money!" Marilyn said with a smirk. Randy laughed.

"That would be nice, but I don't think it's money. It's odd, though ... I sense that someone is trying to lead me somewhere. I know it sounds crazy, but that's the only way I can describe it."

"Randy, nothing you say would surprise me. Things just seem to be getting stranger all the time! I must admit I'm frightened after what took place back on the highway."

"Look, Marilyn, I know you're scared. But like you said, we've got to stick to our plan. Besides, you're the one who brought up the idea of stopping at Hope Cemetery."

Marilyn didn't answer him. In many ways she was thankful that Randy was just as eager to get to the truth of the mystery as she was. It would have been impossible to go on without his encouragement.

Five minutes later they arrived at the huge cemetery. After passing through the entrance, an uneasy feeling began to descend upon Randy. He tried to ignore it.

"Where should we begin looking?" he asked Marilyn, his tone of voice now subdued.

With her eyes scanning the gravestones, Marilyn responded with a measure of uncertainty.

"What are our chances of ever finding the graves without information from the office? Look around, Randy, this place is huge ... it's like looking for a needle in a haystack!" Reluctantly, he agreed.

Continuing their drive through the cemetery they soon reached the end of a dirt pathway. Randy had to turn the station wagon around, taking a right turn onto a dirt road just around the corner. It was at that precise moment that Marilyn spotted a crow sitting on top of a tombstone. Inscribed on the marker, just underneath the crow's feet, was the name "Hammond."

"Oh, my God!" she screamed out. "Look, Randy, look! It's the Hammond plot!"

His facial features strained and ashen in appearance, he now realized what the inner message had meant. There it was, on the side of the road! This must be where it all led.

They got out of the car to take a closer look. The crow didn't budge as they slowly approached the gray, moss-covered tombstone. Henry Hammond's date of death etched out the chilling reality, just as his obituary had ... "Died, January 6 1899." The date on the tombstone confirmed the date in the story.

There was another hair-raising sight, too. Neatly arranged at the top of Henry's headstone was a small pumpkin, a few sea shells, and a piece of quartz crystal, the same array of articles Linda had found sitting atop Maria's headstone.

Hammond Family headstone.

Henry - Ida - Aaron headstones.

Marilyn felt terrified but managed to keep her composure. She knew it didn't make any sense. Through their research they had found no direct descendants of Maria Prouty or Henry Hammond, unless she had missed some important pieces of information. She highly doubted that, however. But could it be that someone went to the extreme of altering the facts that pertained to the story? It was certainly possible, she thought. After all, it seemed apparent that the trail of six "suicides" had been covered up. If certain individuals could get away with that, they could get away with altering birth certificates so as to hide any clues leading to a direct descendant.

As she turned her thoughts to the scene before them, she was suddenly startled. The menacing crow, which up to this time had been resting atop the headstone, spread his wings, lifted off and landed only a few feet away from where they were standing. Seconds later, the skies opened up and cold rain, along with fear, chilled both of them like the blackness of an icy winter's night. As they stood shivering, they now both knew instinctively that the story was surrounded by evil. Was it some kind of message? Surely God would protect them! They were only searching for the truth. But their quest was about to take another bizarre turn.

Randy, as if possessed, suddenly dropped to his knees, reached out and grasped Aaron Hammond's tombstone with both hands.

"Randy, what the hell are you doing? This isn't funny!" Marilyn yelled. "Please don't do this, Randy!"

Randy never heard her. He was somewhere else, listening to something that kept him in rapt attention. Wherever and whatever it was, it was totally unknown and inaudible to her. She wanted to run, to escape the horrifying entity that was taking over her husband. Why couldn't they let go of this dreadful story? How could four people be possessed by its terrible secret?

After what seemed like an eternity, Randy came out of his temporary encounter with the unknown.

Rising to his feet, wearing a mask of uncertainty, he began to explain what he saw in that moment of unconsciousness.

"I could see Henry's face at the very moment he was shot! He was taken by surprise. He looked up from where he was standing beside his desk. I could see the fear in his face. I stared into his eyes, seeing the mirror of his soul vanish into blackness as his assailant ended his life. Henry had no escape. He was unsuspecting of any wrong-doing, and he knew and loved the person that took his life!"

Randy now looked more intently at Marilyn and continued.

"I couldn't see the face of the person who fired the weapon ... I could only see a hand pulling the trigger. But I knew it was Aaron."

"How can you be so sure of that?" Marilyn asked.

"I don't know ... I just see things!" he answered. "I can't explain how it happens ... there's no logical explanation for it at all. The whole thing is too damn weird."

He paused to refocus his thoughts, but at that moment something caught his attention.

"Look, Marilyn!" he shouted.

She watched his hand rise and looked in the direction where he was pointing. A few yards away, just far enough out of their reach, the crow was skulking about the ground, cawing as though it was trying to tell them something. With this, Marilyn ran to the car. Randy followed.

Once they were safely inside, they watched the crow fly back to the Hammond plot.

"Never in my wildest imagination would I have thought a crow would have led us here!" Marilyn confessed. "It's just another bizarre twist."

"I can just see Dave's and Linda's faces when we tell them this one!" Randy replied in amusement. "But maybe we shouldn't tell them."
Marilyn agreed.

As they departed the crow was still perched in the same spot playing keeper of his domain. Marilyn bid the bird a silent thank you. The creature ruffled its feathers as if it understood her thoughts.

SEVEN

With the strange unexplained turn of events rapidly unfolding before them, the irony of the whole situation only intensified their desire to come to some conclusion in their search for the truth. What they had waited for most was about to happen.

Monday afternoon, 4:30 p.m. Marilyn and Linda were on their way to see the Prouty mansion. Both were overwhelmed with the thought of having an opportunity to view the place where Maria had once lived.

Marilyn parked the car across the street from the estate. As they began their walk up to the door, Linda's imagination went into high gear. She wondered if the lion statues, which were perched on both sides of the entrance, were actually the guardians of the mansion's secrets. A few seconds later she returned to the reality at hand.

Viewing their surroundings carefully, both women tried to capture every detail, including the site of the church steeple only a few yards away, with its golden clock soaring upward from behind the hill, pillaring to the sky. This was the very church in which Henry and Iris were to be wed almost a century ago.

Now, at last, the moment they had waited for. Eleanor Cole, standing at the side entrance, graciously greeted them and invited them inside. She led both women directly into the kitchen. Her parents and fiancé were visiting and were seated in two of the elegant kitchen chairs. Eleanor's family knew beforehand the reason for Linda and Marilyn's visit. Her parents seemed amused with the idea of a book possibly being written about the people who once occupied their daughter's home. They were very receptive to Marilyn and Linda, offering to assist with the grand tour of Ashcroft.

Eleanor pointed out that the previous owners had remodeled the kitchen.

"It's obvious they didn't keep the Victorian era in mind for this room," Eleanor mentioned.

Both nodded in agreement as they followed her toward a hallway which led to a Victorian-style dining room that had been meticulously preserved. Off to the right was another hallway that connected to a parlor. This was highlighted by a fireplace trimmed with marble.

Linda found herself staring into the mirror above the mahogany mantel. The voices of Marilyn and the others were now fading as she realized she had been in this room before, the same room in which she had heard the terrible screams. She felt frightened, almost breathless from terror, knowing everything she was seeing in this room was the same as in her dream. The vision of Maria Prouty's last desperate attempt to escape her assailant as she helplessly ran down the hallway toward the front entrance. The dreadful imagery was unfolding in Linda's mind with such detail that she felt a coldness surround her. But as quick as the images appeared, they were gone. Abruptly she was brought back to the reality of Eleanor's conversation concerning the Prouty years.

Linda followed Eleanor and the others through a hallway around a corner. She was confident that she would see the winding staircase just the way it appeared in her dreams. Eleanor continued talking but Linda could no longer hear her.

"What's going on? Where are the stairs that belong here? I saw them!" Linda was insistent.

"What do you mean?" Eleanor asked.

Linda didn't answer. Everyone stared.

Linda sensed what they were thinking but she didn't care. She knew every detail of the mansion, and what she saw now was not right.

Looking quite confused, Eleanor asked, "How would you know about the stairs?"

Marilyn tried to explain but Linda refused to let her help with the awkward situation. She was beyond embarrassment. To her it didn't matter what these people thought of her outburst. She needed answers.

"I've been in this mansion before!" explained Linda, choking with emotion.

With a puzzled look Eleanor asked, "When was that?"

"I've been here through my dreams," Linda said.

A long silence followed. Eleanor and her mother exchanged looks of disbelief.

"Through your dreams?" Eleanor questioned.

"It's hard to explain," Marilyn interjected. "We would like to keep it confidential for now."

"Well, Linda is right," Eleanor confessed. "The staircase to the second floor used to wind its way into the front hallway foyer. The previous owners shortened it in order to hide it behind a wall."

Hearing this bit of information confirmed to Linda that her dreams had given her true insight into the past, right down to the staircase she saw in her nightmares.

On the second floor of the mansion were the bedrooms. They each were furnished with finely restored Victorian furniture. The windows were highlighted with lacy white curtains that draped delicately over a background of wallpaper, bringing to mind a bygone era.

Before they began their tour of the attic, Eleanor called her fiancé, Robert, to join them. As Robert came up the stairs, Eleanor was attempting to open the old door that led to the room above.

"It takes a man's touch for this, Robert. The door is sticking ... I can't open it myself," Eleanor told him candidly.

"Makes you wonder how a frail lady like Maria Prouty opened it!" Marilyn replied.

Robert pulled and tugged on the door. It finally opened.

They ventured up the darkened stairs and wandered into the large shadowed, cavernous chamber. Eleanor and her parents looked on as Marilyn and Linda, both in silence, carefully searched the rafters for hooks or other protruding objects from which a person could tie a rope. They remembered that Chief McKenna had done this almost a century ago. Like him, they found nothing.

They then turned to Eleanor and told her that it was virtually impossible for a lady in such ill health as Maria to have made her way to the attic, without assistance, to commit suicide by hanging.

Linda secretly knew her dream mirrored Maria Prouty's murder. The woman had not met with her demise in the attic – that was a charade designed to mask her murder.

After making their way down the steps and back into the parlor, Marilyn pointed to a turn-of-the-century photograph of a man in his early twenties. The picture sat on a small oval table near the fireplace.

Eleanor responded to Marilyn's gesture by telling her, "That's a picture of a distant relative."

Marilyn didn't press for a name nor did Eleanor volunteer one. She casually turned toward the hallway and asked them to accompany her to the adjoining room.

Marilyn remained alone in the hall for a moment, silenced by her thoughts. For her, the hourglass of time seemed to stop, and in that instant, flickering shadows from the past revealed visions of Iris receiving the shocking news of Henry's death. The room still echoed with Iris's tormented cries. In her heart she did not want to believe the man she loved more than life itself was dead. Iris's world would never be the same.

As Marilyn's thoughts turned to the present, she became filled with sorrow, her eyes welling with tears. She knew she was actually experiencing Iris's grief. She was very uncomfortable with the brief encounter and desperately wanted out of the immediate situation.

Realizing that was not possible, she tried to compose herself. Being drawn back into the conversation at hand in the next room, she wondered how much time had lapsed. Seeing details from the past which foreshadowed the events of the present gave her clear insight into the fantastic mystery. She also questioned herself if it were possible that she was experiencing a connection to a past life. She quickly pushed the thought from her mind and joined the others in the library.

Being somewhat forward, Linda questioned Eleanor about the possibility of the house being haunted. Marilyn was also curious, for once she entered the mansion, she too became privy to the secrets that had been hidden for so long.

With an amused look Eleanor responded calmly to Linda's question.

"No, I've never seen or heard anything in the house, other than the usual creaking that one might hear in an older home."

Marilyn felt Eleanor was not being absolutely honest with them.

Drawing in a deep breath, Linda asked her, "Would you allow us to come back with a photographer?"

Eleanor paused for a minute. "Whom do you have in mind?" she asked.

"John ... I can't think of his last name. He owns the photo shop down the street. He does beautiful work. You probably know him."

"Oh, yes, I've been to the shop many times. I don't have a problem with that. There is one thing, though. I would really like to view the pictures."

Linda looked at Marilyn. They nodded their heads in agreement.

"We'll let you know as soon as they are developed," replied Marilyn.

"After all, you've been kind enough to give us this opportunity to see Ashcroft."

After they arranged a tentative date for their return with the photographer, Linda and Marilyn wished Eleanor well and headed for the door.

A wave of sadness washed over Linda as she exited the grand estate. She felt a sense of personal connection to the mystery. The unearthly events were playing with her emotions, making her feel related to a past that, in some strange way, may have included her in its dark secrets.

Both women hurried to the car without saying a word to each other. Once inside, Marilyn reached for her sole vice. Linda watched her friend nervously light the cigarette and inhale. She then quickly exhaled as if she were trying to cough up something foul.

Marilyn carefully checked the rear-view mirror before pulling away from the curb and driving back down Ash Street. In the animated discussion that ensued both women compared notes on what they had each experienced while inside the mansion. They couldn't come up with any rational explanation for feeling the way they did, yet they couldn't simply ignore it and write off the unexplained phenomena as mere fantasies. They needed to concentrate on what had to be done.

They were being drawn deeper and deeper into the web of the Prouty-Hammond enigma. There was no escaping the fact that many unusual things had occurred, and this only served to urge them on in their investigation.

In the days ahead they found themselves discussing McKenna's theories about the deaths and how all the victims' lives came to abrupt ends, all within a month's time. To Dave it defied all logic.

Reading over the information they got from the library, they began putting more pieces together.

EIGHT

The Pinkerton National Detective Agency had offices in all major cities in the country. The Boston office had a branch office located in the Park Building, 1106 Main Street, Worcester. The branch's agent-in-charge was Franklin W. Adams, a cousin to the Adams family in Spencer. Franklin Adams was a business associate and friend of Aaron Hammond, and the two men were often seen lunching together in several of Worcester's fine eateries. Also whenever Hammond traveled by rail to the Midwest to review shipping policies, Adams would arrange to have Pinkerton agents from Worcester accompany him.

McKenna knew that Frank Berry's body had been discovered by Pinkerton agents in Louisiana. It would have been the agents' duty to report the death to local police authorities. But had the Pinkerton Agency in Louisiana also notified Aaron Hammond of Frank Berry's murder? McKenna wondered about this. He also thought about how Aaron Hammond had connections that reached out over the entire country. The power and wealth of this self-made man was becoming more evident as his investigation continued. He began to realize that money, together with power, was the dominant force in what he perceived was an elaborate coverup.

While McKenna was having a drink with Will McDonald at the bar in the Massasoit Hotel, he told the reporter what he thought might have happened. He went on to explain ...

"Frank Berry gets paid to deliver a message to Henry Hammond. Berry gets scared off and can't go through with it. He keeps the money and runs. He heads to Louisiana. By the time he gets there, Hammond's hired thugs are already waiting to put an end to him. That took care of his ever telling anyone about the message he was to deliver to Henry."

McDonald listened raptly as the chief continued.

"Then Aaron recruits Albert Nichols to do the job. But Nichols figures that Aaron is responsible for his friend's suicide. In some way George Dumas and John Taylor also knew something about the fatal message. Aaron then hires George Dumas, surmising that he knows about the hidden secret of the message. John Taylor and Frank Berry had met in Boston to discuss the situation."

McKenna sensed that the conniving duo put the scheme together and somehow made Dumas part of the plot.

"I was told by Harris Dodge," McKenna confided, "that a mystery woman was seen accompanying Aaron Hammond on his business trips to Charlton. It could very well have been Maria Prouty. You know, there is a possibility that Iris was Aaron's illegitimate daughter."

Dear God, McDonald thought, this would make Henry and Iris half brother and sister! The pieces of the puzzle were finally falling into place.

McKenna sipped his beer, looked at McDonald and asked, "To what lengths would Aaron go to prevent this wedding if he knew he was Iris's father? What reaction would William Prouty have once he found out about it?"

Suddenly everything seemed to fit. Could this have been the fatal message, McKenna wondered. To prove it, however, would be a different matter. Maybe Frank Berry told John Taylor and George Dumas about the message and with that information Taylor and Dumas devised a plan to blackmail Aaron Hammond. Their plan backfired, leading to their own deaths. How far would a desperate man go to keep his dirty secrets? Murder certainly was not out of the question. As for Maria, once William was informed of the affair, he went into a jealous rage, and in a fit of anger he killed her. What about the anonymous note sent to McKenna's office revealing that Aaron Hammond and Maria Prouty were seen in a heated argument near a wooded area of Chartlon, just after the announcement of Henry and Iris's wedding?

McKenna now felt that, with this bit of knowledge, he was only steps away from the truth.

But he was in for a rude awaking. He soon learned that the town fathers agreed to press the selectmen to force both police departments to terminate their investigations.

Meeting with McDonald again a few days later, he told the reporter, "If you know the right people in this town, you can get away with murder! This group of wealthy bastards ... one lies and the other swears to it."

NINE

After reviewing the article and the discussing the implications of McKenna's theories, the two couples knew they needed more information if they wanted to put faces to the names of the main characters. The closest they had come were sketches of Henry Hammond, Iris, Maria and William Prouty. There had to be more pictures somewhere, although none had turned up at the library. But they did have the one thing that no one else knew about – the gun! Yet this was their only evidence so far. More needed to be found.

It was Saturday night, and instead of making plans for her and her husband's customary night out at their favorite restaurant, Marilyn called Linda and asked if both she and Dave would come by a little later in the evening. Linda agreed, indicating that both she and Dave were not doing much that evening anyway.

Seating themselves around the dining room table, each waited for the other to begin the review of where the investigation had taken them so far.

Marilyn was the first to speak. Stretching her arms out in front of her, her eyes cast downward, she began the discussion.

"I think we should talk with someone who is experienced with past life regression. As much as I hate to admit it, I think we need to seek the advice of a psychic."

When Marilyn looked up, she couldn't help notice how Linda was nervously twisting strands of her raven-colored hair, her eyes wide with disbelief.

"Look," Marilyn continued, "before anyone has a chance to voice his or her opinion here, let me tell you about Ted Rabouin, the psychic."

With raised eyebrows and a look of recognition in his face, Dave replied, "I've heard that name before ... I believe *Worcester Magazine* did a story about him in the early 1970s."

"That's right," said Marilyn.

Dave continued. "The article was printed on Halloween. I was rummaging through some boxes in the cellar the other day when I came across it. I also remember reading that he had been a guest on several talk shows. They said he was the founder of the First Church of Wicca, and he was its high priest!"

"No way!" Linda asserted. "That's devil worship ... don't get us involved!"

"Calm down, Linda," Dave interrupted. "He is supposed to be the best psychic around. The police even use his services. I don't see anything wrong with talking to him. If we show him the gun, maybe he would agree to help us."

"Why don't we give it a try?" Marilyn asked.

Randy leaned back against his chair, his forehead wrinkled with concern. He stared at Dave and said, "I guess it would be okay if it gave us some insight to the story, but unfortunately I have to admit that I'm not comfortable with the idea of a psychic. However, I can't come up with a better suggestion."

"All right, since it was my idea I'll make the call," Marilyn said.

"This goes against everything I believe in!" Linda added uneasily. "I want to make sure you all understand I'm dead set against this idea!"

"Linda, there's nothing to worry about ... just consider it research," Marilyn retorted.

With a chuckle Dave replied, "Well, Marilyn, you'd better call Mr. Rabouin to set up an appointment before everyone changes their minds." Randy nodded, agreeing with Dave.

Marilyn scanned the white pages of the telephone book, her eyes roaming up and down the columns for the name "Rabouin." At the same time she tried to think of what she would say to the man should she reach him.

"Rabouin, Rabouin ... this must be him!" she shouted as her fingers fell upon the name, the only one listed for Westboro.

"You've found his number?" Randy asked.

She didn't answer. Her hands shook and her heart pounded as she reached for a pen to copy it down. Without saying a word she walked over to the phone in the kitchen. The receiver felt heavy as she lifted it from its sleek, almond-colored cradle. She secretly hoped he wouldn't answer. She was as afraid of the idea as the others were – far be it from her to let them know.

After only two rings someone picked up. She felt the perspiration weep from the pores of her skin.

"Ah, hello ... is Mr. Rabouin home?" she asked.

"Yes, this is he. How may I help you?"

He didn't sound at all like what she'd expected. Then she thought, what did she expect him to sound like anyway? Actually he had a pleasant voice.

"I would like to set up an appointment for my husband, two friends, and myself to meet with you," Marilyn asked him cautiously.

"Is this for a reading?" Rabouin replied.

Marilyn insisted that she was not calling for a reading.

"We've come across an old revolver," she explained, "and we were wondering if you would be able to tell us if the weapon had been used in a crime."

He chuckled. "Well, my dear, I want to tell you it's been some time since I've done that sort of thing." After a pause he resumed. "To say the least, I do like a good mystery, and if there is one that comes with this gun, I'll be sure to find it for you. I'm available Monday evening. If you and your friends can come over around 7:30, I'll be happy to talk with you."

Marilyn appreciated the confident tone in his voice.

After confirming the appointment, she asked for directions to his home. He told her to drive to Westboro center and then call him from a pay phone there. He would then give her explicit directions at that time. She agreed. With a quick motion she hung up the phone and breathed a nervous sigh of relief.

"Well, where does he live?" Randy asked impatiently.

"We have to call him when we get to Westboro center Monday evening," replied Marilyn.

With a puzzled look Linda asked, "What do you mean? Why did he ask you to call from there?"

"Think about it, Linda ... put yourself in his shoes for a minute. We have a gun and we want to come to your home. How would you feel if four strangers wanted to enter your house with a weapon? I'm sure that's why he didn't give us specific directions at this time."

"Do you think he'll feel differently about our meeting him when we make the call from Westboro center this coming Monday," Linda asked smugly.

"We'll find out Monday night, won't we?" Marilyn told her, seemingly annoyed. "I can only tell you what he told me."

Dave, remaining quiet up to this point, broke into the conversation.

"Okay, let's take it easy. I think we're all a bit edgy. Maybe we should sleep on this. You ladies have a big week ahead of you. You'll be going back to Ashcroft with the photographer, and after that you have a psychic to visit. I think the excitement that this story is generating is wearing on your nerves."

They all agreed. It was time to call it a night.

The following afternoon Marilyn, Linda, and John, the photographer, began their short journey to the Prouty mansion. Along the way Marilyn told John about the photo she saw on the small antique table in the parlor, just to the left of the fireplace. Something about the portrait intrigued her, and she asked John if he would take a picture of it. He assured her he would. She couldn't understand why she was drawn to it. She wondered if she was attracted to the young man's handsome good looks. His eighteenth-century apparel clearly represented wealth, but she knew there was something more. His dark, deep-set eyes seemed to hide something. His features were similar to those in the sketch of young Henry as he appeared on the front page of the story that Bobby had found. It was uncanny.

"Well, here we are," Linda announced. They were ready for their second tour of Ashcroft.

Eleanor was waiting by the side door when they approached. After Marilyn introduced John they entered the grand foyer and headed for the staircase. When they reached the second floor John noticed that he was having trouble with his camera.

"That's strange," he said.

"What's the matter, John?" asked Linda.

"It takes two buttons to shut my camera off, " he explained. "It shut off twice in the bedroom when I was trying to take a picture. I've never had that happen before ... in fact, it's impossible!"

Linda and Marilyn exchanged uneasy glances.

"Were you able to get any pictures?" Linda asked.

"Yes, I got some," John said, still looking a bit baffled. "I just don't understand why my camera suddenly quit on me like that. It doesn't make any sense."

Eleanor remained quiet while she watched John inspect the camera. He looked at the lens, turned the buttons on and off, and checked the other settings carefully, trying to find a reason for the problem. He found nothing wrong and this irked him.

The tour was now at an end. Eleanor led them downstairs, back into the foyer and then outside. Linda and Marilyn thanked her for being so accommodating.

John began walking the grounds taking more pictures. Linda and Marilyn joined him at the bottom of the driveway where he was attempting to focus his camera on the church steeple in the distance.

"Well, considering what's been happening," he said, "I was still able to get you some good pictures. But I'm still baffled about this!"

Marilyn raised her brow, and with a very serious expression on her face, informed him, "Don't be surprised by this, John ... I'm sure you'll find nothing wrong with your camera. Linda and I have been experiencing a lot of strange, unexplainable things lately."

Looking concerned he responded, "I know ... Linda told me all about it, but I ..."

Linda immediately interrupted him. "But you found it hard to believe, didn't you?"

"I promise to have the pictures ready, pronto," he said, ignoring her question. "I'm going right to the photo shop from here, and I want to get these developed right away. I'm as anxious to see them as you are. Meet me at the shop around nine o'clock this evening. The place will be closed at that time and we won't be interrupted."

Later that evening the four friends had a lengthy conversation over dinner. Discussing the day's unusual events took up most of their time, but trying to put things into perspective took them even longer. Their once normal world had abandoned them, replacing reality with the world of the unknown, leaving them with only each other to turn to for support. They knew that no one else would believe them.

The four of them met with John at nine o'clock as planned. He looked a bit solemn as Marilyn reached for the packet of photos he had in his hand. She hesitated before opening it.

"Did you see any ghost in the photos?" Marilyn jokingly asked him.

146

John became somewhat pale. In a serious tone of voice, and without as much as a blink, he replied, "Why don't you look for yourself?"

The others were silent and watched Marilyn's laugh quickly fade. Huddling together they carefully sorted through the photos, one by one, not really sure of what they were looking for. It was obvious that John saw something while developing the film. The photo of the picture of the young man which Marilyn requested John to take was on top.

Randy was the first to speak.

"Where did you get this picture of Henry Hammond?" They all looked.

"Yeah, you would swear it was him," Marilyn replied.

"You mean it's not?" Randy questioned.

"We're sure it is but we can't prove it," Marilyn confessed. "Eleanor was very tight-lipped about it. That's one of the reasons I was so intrigued by the photo, plus its uncanny likeness to the sketch."

"I wonder if she's related?" Randy asked.

"I don't know what to make of it," Marilyn replied. "And since we have no way of finding out, I guess it will remain a mystery."

"Hey, look at this!" Linda shouted. "Look at the picture that was taken from the front of the house. Do you see the bedroom window?"

In unison their eyes were drawn to an image of someone staring out the window, the window of the very room that Maria Prouty had called her own. It appeared to be an outline of a woman, her hair swept back in a bun, her clothing in the fashion of the century gone by. A morbid feeling cast itself over Linda. She couldn't quite believe her eyes. Yet, still there was more! She was now looking at another picture that was taken from inside the bedroom. In it was a poster bed draped with a white comforter, and laying across the spread was a white scarf. She knew it wasn't there when John took the picture. Linda also distinctly remembered that the room was immaculate and that nothing was out of place.

Marilyn then turned to John for an answer.

"Would it be possible for the sun, as it streamed through the window, to cast a shadow in such a way as to create the effect of something lying on the bed?"

"Yes, it's very possible," said John. "The image we see in the window could even be coming from a tree near the house. It just depends on the time of day the photo was taken."

Marilyn thought about it for a minute. What time does the sun go down? Why would the shadow on the bed be in the shape of a scarf? What made the image in the window appear to be that of a woman from the Victorian era? What kind of a coincidence could this be?

Leaning against the counter she asked, "Weren't we at Ashcroft around 4:30?"

"Yes, it was 6:15 p.m. when we left the estate," John replied.

"How do you remember the exact time?" she asked.

"When we walked outside I took a picture of the church. If you look at the clock on the steeple, you'll see the time is 6:15 p.m."

Randy was now clearly interested.

"The wedding ceremony was scheduled for 6:00 ... the deaths occurred at 6:00 ... and there were six murders!" he blurted out. "Does anyone else find it strange that the number 'six' shows up quite often, or is it my imagination?"

No one answered. The initial shock of seeing what the photos showed was enough to make the four of them question once again the reasons for continuing with their quest.

Was this yet another link in the chain that kept them searching for the truth behind the mysterious deaths?

The Prouty Mansion as it is today. Notice the strange image in the upper left front window of the mansion. At the time this picture was taken there was nothing in the window. There is no logical explanation for the ghostly image

This is what we believe to be Maria Prouty's bedroom. When this photograph was taken, there were no articles of any type on the bed. You'll notice in this picture there is a ladys scarf draped across the bed. Also notice the flash unit on the camera caused a shadow to form, the shadow does not penetrate the scarf.

The living room of the Prouty Mansion as it is today.

This is the stairwell to the 2nd floor and the attic where Maria Prouty supposedly took her own life.

TEN

A few days would lapse before they would embark once again on their investigative journey. Monday evening might have come too soon for them, had they each not searched their souls and hoped they were doing the right thing.

The bristle blue sky from early afternoon had changed into an evening gray overcast. It was threatening rain as they made their way down the exit ramp heading into Westboro. A few miles down Route 9 led them to the center of town where they saw the array of franchise businesses that one would expect to see in all towns, each with its famous signage bathed in garish colors. Their search for a telephone booth took them to the brightly lit pink and white neon that surrounded the Dunkin' Donuts shop.

When they opened the car doors the irresistible smell of coffee and pastry lured Marilyn and Linda inside, leaving Randy and Dave to make the call to Mr. Rabouin. After purchasing a few choice pastries, which they hoped to enjoy later in the evening, they hurried outside only to find themselves in a sudden drenching downpour. Randy and Dave were waiting in the car which was parked directly out front. Both women made a mad dash to the gray Lincoln, trying desperately to avoid getting soaked.

When they were safely inside Marilyn immediately sensed something was wrong. It was obvious by the look on Randy's face that the phone call to Mr. Rabouin had left him feeling uncomfortable.

"What's wrong?" she asked him.

Dave interrupted Randy before he had a chance to answer.

"We're off to find a gingerbread house!" Dave said with a smirk.

"You're joking!" Marilyn exclaimed, not understanding the meaning.

"I wish he was," Randy answered.

Linda's eyes widened.

"Oh, no!" she cried out. "Let's just turn around and forget the whole thing!"

Dave, now seemingly annoyed, replied, "Don't be foolish, Linda!"

It was no surprise to her that Dave hadn't been drawn completely into the mysteries that she, Marilyn, and Randy were trying to solve. He was trying to downplay the apparent weirdness of the recent events, rationalizing that one of them had to play the devil's advocate.

After leaving the donut shop they drove back to the Route 9 on-ramp. Silence slipped its way into the car and wrapped itself around each of them. They were all thinking about how their lives had been turned upside down in the last few months. A whispering voice seemed to loom over their thoughts, and with their imaginations growing ever wilder, it planted a question in their minds about Mr. Rabouin and what he might look like.

Each one pictured him differently. Randy had a strong feeling that he wore glasses. For some reason he felt the glasses were either of the wrong prescription or were broken. It didn't make sense to him why he would think this, but then again a lot of things didn't make sense these days.

The sound of thunder and the hard-driving rain beating against the car hampered their search for Bowman Street.

"What's the number on the house?" Linda asked.

In a sarcastic tone, Dave replied, "I don't remember ... just look for a gingerbread house, okay?"

Dave was getting a bit edgy. Linda and her friends knew he thought that all of this was nothing but nonsense. They accepted the fact and thought it best not to try to persuade him differently.

Bowman Street now loomed dead ahead, and as they approached the street corner, there stood the house. One couldn't possibly miss it – it looked like a scene from the Hansel and Gretel fable.

"Dave! Dave! Watch out! What the hell are you doing? You're going to get us all killed!" Randy shouted.

Dave gripped the steering wheel and pulled the car to the right. He had swerved into the opposite lane of the small, winding country road, just missing an oncoming van.

Sounding scared and a bit out of breath, he apologized to the others. "Sorry!" he confessed. "I was looking at the house. I couldn't help it ... I wasn't paying attention when we came around the bend. I spotted the place, and if I hadn't seen it with my own eyes, I wouldn't have believed it!"

Dave was still apologizing as he put the car into reverse and backed into the pea-stone driveway. To the left of the house was a white Victorian gazebo equipped with a small round table draped with a lace tablecloth. On top was a very old-fashioned lamp. Attached to the lattice that bordered the dainty structure was a large Jack O'Lantern, the eyes on its painted face staring boldly into the darkness. The autumn leaves were scattered about the yard. Across the way, on the porch, several cats were lying about. The windows had paintings of white curtains on them. The whole scene gave the appearance of a perfect Halloween night.

As they walked over to take a closer look, Marilyn remarked, "It must be easy to do your spring and fall cleaning this way ... everything gets washed at the same time!" The funny comment helped ease some of the tension they were all feeling.

"Here goes!" Randy said.

Stepping onto the small front porch, his knees wobbling, he knocked on the front door. Certainly he had been in more frightening situations than this! The jungles of Vietnam's Mekong Delta had definitely taken their toll on him – so why was he feeling so vulnerable now?

The old creaking wooden door opened. The man in the hallway was slightly overweight and was dressed in a comfortable-looking jogging suit. His hair was gray and a tad mussed.

With a smooth, deep voice he said, "Good evening, I'm Ted Rabouin. Please do come in."

Linda was wringing her hands while the introductions were being made. After a few minutes inside the picturesque cottage she began to feel the warmth of the blazing fire coming from the pot-bellied wood stove.

Marilyn noticed that the platform on which the stove sat was, of all things, a tombstone. Nudging Randy, she discreetly tried to turn his attention to the hearth by raising her brows and shifting her gaze in its direction. Randy followed her silent gestures. When he spotted the unusual fixture, a frown appeared across his forehead and he shifted his body nervously.

Their gaze was interrupted when Mr. Rabouin invited all of them to join him in the reading room. He led them past the kitchen which was decorated like an illustration straight out of a child's storybook. A ceramic strawberry shortcake, three layers thick, was sitting on top of an old-fashioned cooking oven. It all gave the appearance of something you would have expected to see at your grandmother's house when you were a child.

From the kitchen they followed him through a dark hallway into a beautiful Victorian-style parlor. The ambiance of the room reflected a bygone era. The marble tables and the delicate-looking velvet furnishings gave a feeling of warmth which, to their surprise, they had not expected. It certainty fit with the theme of their story. The nineteenth-century surroundings made them feel comfortable.

Mr. Rabouin sensed they were impressed with his choice of furnishings.

"I picked up a lot of my antiques at flea markets," he said as he surveyed the contents of the room. "As you can see, I have a passion for all things old and unique."

He then turned his attention to them.

"Well, if you folks will have a seat, I will join you in a moment ... I'd like to get a cold drink before we start. Would any of you like an ice tea or soda?"

They declined his kind offer, and with that, he excused himself and hurried off to the kitchen.

Suddenly a pair of brown Chihuahuas made their presence known. Begging for attention, they began to jump around and sniff at the intruders.

"Babies! Babies!" he called. "I see my little ones are checking you out."

Entering the room, he shuffled past the dogs with his drink in hand, trying to be careful not to fall. Marilyn smiled and reached down to pet one of the animals, but they all swiftly scurried from her reach, jumping up into the overstuffed chair to join their master.

As Mr. Rabouin cradled himself into the chair, the ice in his beverage clinked against the inside of the glass. A few drops of the caramel-colored liquid swished over the rim and spilled into his lap. He laughed.

"I'm afraid I've been a bit clumsy the last few weeks ... I've been having trouble with my eyes. I think it's time for new glasses."

Randy felt his stomach turn as he began to remember the thoughts he had about Mr. Rabouin during the ride to the cottage. What led him to think about this man's problem with his eyeglasses, of all things! Why would he sense that? Shaking the thought from his mind, he turned his attention to what was being said.

Mr. Rabouin began.

"Well, folks, I think it's time for me to see what you've brought."

Linda was sitting on the edge of her chair, her blue leather pocketbook clutched tightly in her hands. All eyes were on her as she carefully used both hands to remove the revolver from her bag. With the gun lying sideways, she cradled it in her palms. Rising from her chair she cautiously carried it over to where Mr. Rabouin was seated. Leaning down she extended her hands and presented it to him.

He touched it and winced, sucking his breath in just enough for them to see his chest heave.

"Death! Death! The gun has brought death," he whispered.

Dave, seated only a few feet away from Mr. Rabouin, looked across to his wife and friends, rolling his eyes to show them he was not impressed. Nonetheless, they ignored him, wanting to hear more from the renowned psychic.

Mr. Rabouin continued.

"First I have to prepare you. I will say things that will make sense to you ... and some of what I talk about will mean nothing to you. Take what you need, leave the rest. One more thing ... call me by my first name, Teddy."

With his eyes closed, he rubbed the barrel of the gun. He seemed to enter another time dimension as he began thrusting words and sentences together.

"Darkness, I see a vast darkness ... people feel a desire to know. I hear sinister voices and an organ playing in the distance."

He paused. The silence in the room seemed to go on forever.

"There is a name on the organ but the letters keep fading. If I could just get closer, I would be able to see it."

"Who cares what the name of the organ is," Randy whispered.

"Shush," Marilyn admonished.

Teddy squinted his eyes as he looked into a world that was unknown to most.

"Wait! The letters are getting clearer. The name looks like ... 'Hum' or 'Ham' ... no, no, that's not it. Hammond. It's Hammond!"

Everyone was on the edge of their seats. Dave's arm dropped from a resting position down to his side. The doubt he felt earlier now gave way to total disbelief.

"I see a young man playing the organ. His features are dark ... he's a strikingly handsome young man. I want to say the name Hank, or ..."

He stopped. A dead silence hung in the air. He put his hand over his brow and continued his inner search, calling out the name "Hank" once again.

"What's missing? I know I'm close. Why can't I ... wait, I know, it's coming to me ... Henry, Henry Hammond!" he shouted. "He's the one this gun was used on ... he was killed with it."

The four of them were shocked by the psychic's revelation. How could he know all this by simply touching an old gun?

Dave had an uneasy feeling gnawing at him. His heart pounded as if it were about to explode in his chest. An overpowering sensation of dread tunneled down his throat, right into his gut. He never experienced anything like this, not even in his wildest imaginings. What the hell was going on here? He looked around and tried to focus on the others. The room seemed to spin. He had to get hold of himself before anyone noticed.

"Dave, are you okay?" Marilyn's voice startled him.

Embarrassed, he answered, "I'm fine ... it's just a little hot in here, that's all."

"Maybe you should step outside."

"No, really, I'm okay."

Teddy Rabouin remained quiet, still focusing on the past.

"Two men were shot with this gun!" he called out. "Both were shot dead center, in the forehead. I see the name 'Demers' ... does this name mean anything?"

"Yes," answered an astonished Randy, thinking to himself at the same time how interesting it was that Rabouin had come up with this name, when all along he and the others thought Dumas to be the correct name.

As far as Randy was concerned, this just gave more credibility to Teddy Rabouin's psychic abilities.

Teddy faded deeper into the realms of his unconscious mind. Closing his eyes, he regressed back in time to try to dig into the mystery and its hidden secrets. He then painted for the incredulous foursome very descriptive scenes from the victims' lives.

He kept slipping in and out of muted conversations, transcending time even further, traveling to the past and back again to the present. He told them he could smell a strong odor of lilacs.

"I can see a man climbing into a house ... he's coming in through a first-floor window. I see something in his hand but I can't make out what it is."

The two couples watched Teddy intensely, mesmerized by his running narrative of what he was seeing.

Suddenly his expression changed. As Teddy looked back into the century gone by, he shouted, "It looks like a gun! He has this gun ... the very revolver I have here in front of me! He's wrapping it now in newspaper ... there's another man helping him. I see the name 'Adams', I want to say John Adams ... but I know that was a president's name. Maybe it's Jonas ... no, wait, it's Jason ... Jason Adams. He's hiding the revolver between the slats in a bathroom!"

Teddy's eyes widened. He looked at Dave and asked, "You own the house, don't you?"

Dave couldn't bring himself to answer. He seemed powerless, unable to participate.

Randy handled the situation, answering for Dave, "Yes, he owns the house where the gun was found ... and in back of the house, along the property line, are lilacs."

Teddy smiled. He was pleased that his psychic powers had worked so well for him – right down to smelling the lilacs.

"Unbelievable!" Dave mumbled to his wife.

Teddy looked straight into Dave's eyes and said, "Dave, I know you're very strong-willed and don't want to believe any of this, yet you're baffled by what I've told you. Proving that I have some kind of ability to see into the unknown really disturbs you."

Teddy quickly turned his attention toward Randy who was looking rather pale.

"You're not aware of this," he explained to Randy, "but I want you to know that you have a psychic ability ... it's called precognition. Up until now you've chosen to ignore it, but soon you'll have to confront it. And there's also something else you'll have to deal with ... you will soon learn that the house you were brought up in belonged to one of the murdered victims!"

Randy felt his body surge forward. For a moment he felt as if he were falling down a steep hill, tumbling aimlessly into a bottomless pit. He wondered what in God's name he was doing in this crazy situation. Marilyn could see the color drain from his face.

They all wondered what their fate would be from this point on. What did the powers from beyond have in store for them?

Teddy had something to tell each one of his visitors. He sat quietly for a few minutes and then asked them – almost demanded them – to get pictures of the Proutys and Hammonds.

"I don't know why right now, but I do know you need to get some photos of these two families," he said.

Marilyn replied, "I have a couple of sketches with me."

Teddy's eyes lit up.

"I know the face of the killer," he told her. "I'll be able to pick him out for you."

The mere thought of Teddy being able to identify Maria Prouty's assailant had the four of them on the edge of their seats. She reached inside her handbag and took out the unlabeled photos of the sketches of Henry Hammond, Iris, Maria and William. She handed them to Teddy and he began to scrutinize the photos of Henry and William first.

"This is the man ... I would know those eyes anywhere," he shouted. "This man really didn't mean to kill Maria ... it was done in a jealous rage. He lost control!" Teddy was looking at William's photo.

He informed them that William went through life carrying the burden of his guilt and never really had a peaceful day in his life after that. From that day forward William would relive the dreadful scene over and over in his mind, wishing he could have changed it.

Linda thought back to her recurring nightmares. The hands of the faceless individual that she had seen so often must have been those of William Prouty. It brought a chill to her body.

Teddy called out to Linda. She cringed when he said her name, afraid of what he might tell her.

"Linda, you have relatives that worked in the coal mines. One of them was decapitated in an awful accident. He was wearing a scapular that helped identify his body."

She looked over at Dave. They both knew that this man was right, but how could he know all of this? His powerful insight unsettled them.

He continued with his astounding revelations of the events of the past and present.

"Linda, Maria Prouty's pain is reflected in your dreams. She wants the world to know that she did not commit suicide ... her life was taken from her ... and she cannot rest in peace until you tell her story."

"I see a nun standing behind you!" he added.

Linda turned her head to the side, trying to look in back of her to see if anything was there.

"Don't be frightened ... you can't see her. Trust me, she is here to protect you."

"What do I need to be protected from?" Linda said with an anguished tone. "Am I in some kind of danger? You make me feel scared!"

"No need to worry, she won't let any harm come to you."

Linda felt like she had stepped into the cliffhanger scene of an Alfred Hitchcock movie. She was happy to see him finally turn his attention to Marilyn.

"Marilyn, I know you're a non-believer, or I should say that you think you are. However, you really are the strongest believer in this group ... you seek to verify everything before you admit to what you believe. There is nothing wrong with that, except I think you should go with your feelings and see where they take you."

Teddy became silent for a moment, staring at Marilyn. She began to feel intimidated by him.

"What's wrong?" he asked. She said nothing in response.

"Marilyn, you have something from the past. I feel it has something to do with the gun ... where it was found. Am I right?"

"Yes, I have a piece of petrified wood with a painting of Dave's parents' house on it. The house is depicted the way it looked back in the late nineteenth century."

Teddy didn't reply to this bit of news. Instead he said, "I feel drained but I have to continue. I see more ... this is a lot deeper than you think!"

They all looked at each other, wondering what he meant.

"I see a man dressed in judge's robes," he suddenly announced.

Marilyn gasped and leaned over and whispered in Linda's ear, "That has to be Judge Hill!"

Teddy continued with more surprising information gleaned from the dark past, uncovering its secrets, enticing the adventurous group to listen to his every word.

"There's a doctor ... he was a very good friend to all of these prominent people. There was a big coverup ... several botched autopsies. The Proutys, the Hammonds, the judge and this doctor ... all of them were business associates. These men had control of every business interest in Spencer. There were several fraudulent papers signed for this purpose ... but I'm not quite sure of the contents of these documents. Aaron Hammond was the banker behind these schemes ... his wealth afforded him many amenities. I believe he took ... no, I *know* he took his own son's life. It had something to do with incest. I'm trying to get a clearer picture of all this. I'm getting very tired, but I'm so close ... I can't quit now."

Teddy paused, then he continued after taking in a deep breath.

"Aaron had an affair with Maria, and Iris was the result of that affair. Maria never told Aaron until Henry announced his engagement to Iris."

Teddy hesitated, directing his attention toward Marilyn.

"Things just keep coming to me! Maria insisted that Aaron put a stop to the wedding. The outcome ... Henry murdered by his father. Aaron, outraged at what he had to do, informs William Prouty of the affair, knowing that it would bring about the demise of Maria, whom Aaron now loathed. Aaron also banked on the fact that William would never reveal the dark secret, for it would only bring needless pain to Iris."

Teddy paused again, now turning his attention toward Randy.

"Both Hammond and Prouty knew that the good doctor would cover up their indiscretions by ruling suicide in the examiner's report, and then the judge would back up the doctor's findings. After all, Aaron's money was needed to keep the wheels of progress moving, which meant great wealth for all concerned as well as the continuation of their high social standing within the community. Money and power ... the root of all evil!"

What they believed to be the truth of the mystery had now been verified by the keen, though unorthodox, insight of a psychic.

"Are you a religious person?" Teddy asked Marilyn.

Looking a bit bewildered by his question, she was careful to think about how she was going to answer him.

"Well, I have a strong belief in God, if that's what you mean, but I don't attend church on a regular basis. My weekends are taken up with dog shows. I'm an AKC licensed judge."

Abruptly, she put her hands up to her head and buried her face in them. She could not believe she had just disclosed to this man her personal reasons for not attending church. It wasn't any of his business. She was upset with herself. What was his purpose in asking this personal question? She was about to find out.

Teddy became quiet. His face twisted with anger as he turned his attention again towards Marilyn. She felt an ugly situation was about to unfold. He began to speak, and as the others listened in total disbelief, his voice changed to a raspy, belligerent muffle.

"I would like to slap you right across the face!" he told her.

An embarrassing silence floated around the room. Randy and Dave exchanged an uneasy glance which caught Linda's attention, signaling that it was time to get out of there.

Marilyn, however, did not respond. She was staring at Teddy, showing no reaction to what this man had just said.

Immediately after his display of hostility toward Marilyn, Teddy regained his composure and told her how sorry he was.

"That wasn't me talking to you, it was a spirit wanting to stop you from pursuing the truth about the deaths. You must realize that they have successfully concealed these facts for a century ... certainly they don't want the secrets revealed now. They are going to make lots of trouble for you. They have already come to you in your dreams and thoughts ... it's far from over. Be prepared ... you should all say a lot of prayers and attend church. It would be a good idea for each of you to wear a cross."

Marilyn shrugged off Teddy's verbal invasiveness with commendable calm and grace.

"I'm not afraid of any spirits from beyond," she announced.

The others remained quiet, trying to comprehend what they had just heard and witnessed. It seemed that Teddy was showing considerable interest in the Prouty-Hammond saga, treating it with a deep concern, almost as if he knew something was going to happen, something that Dave, Linda, Marilyn and Randy were not prepared for.

Two hours had passed. He was still astounding the foursome with unbelievable descriptions of the events of the victims' lives.

Randy was now comfortable with the fact that this man had definitely proved he was not an impostor. It would have been impossible for him to come up with some of the details he had unveiled to them, including certain details about their own lives. Randy felt it was important to tell Teddy about the ornaments that were being left on the graves of Henry Hammond and Maria Prouty. Maybe he would have some insight into this madness.

"The items you've described to me are the paraphernalia of witchcraft," he explained to them.

Marilyn and Linda quickly glanced at each other. They didn't want to tell Teddy that they, had suspicions that there may have been a child born of the affair of Iris and Henry.

Teddy changed the subject.

"It is very important for both of you to visit the Prouty mansion," he advised them.

"We've been there twice already," Marilyn informed him. "We may go back but we're not sure at this point."

"You must have seen or felt the presence of Maria's spirit ... she lives there!"

Both Linda and Marilyn remained silent about their experience, guarding their knowledge and feelings about the mansion in sacred trust.

Teddy pressed on as if he knew.

"If you remember what I told you earlier about the spirits, it is not unusual to be visited by them. I wish I could go with you to the Prouty estate, but I've been very sick lately and I need to get plenty of rest."

It was obvious to them that he was not a well man.

He became very solemn. Closing his eyes and searching deep within himself he spoke again.

"Damn it, I just know that mansion holds many of the answers you're looking for. If only I could get inside ... I know I can reach Maria's spirit. I know Maria's soul still lives there. I desperately need to speak with her. This woman who owns the mansion today ... mark my words, she knows that Maria is in that house ... I know she has seen Maria for herself. I want you ladies to be careful ... never let her become aware that I told you any of this. Observe everything ... let nothing escape you. It's there for your taking if you know what to look for."

At this point, Teddy requested they stop. He had revealed many things to them throughout the course of the evening, and now he was exhausted.

The foursome began to make their way to the door.

"Keep in contact with me and, if necessary, I will see you again," Teddy told them just as they were about to step outside. He then put his hand on Randy's shoulder and reminded him, "I told you earlier this evening that you have psychic abilities, a sixth sense ... learn how to use it, but be very careful!"

Randy didn't say a word, but it was obvious from his expression that he was left somewhat dismayed by Teddy's warning. He knew he had experienced some bizarre thoughts lately, particularly the image that seemed to pulsate inside his head – the image of finding something along the side of the road. He wondered if that could be what Teddy meant about his having a sixth sense. Or was it just coincidental?

During the ride back to Spencer Randy was intent on trying to figure out which murdered victim had once occupied the home he was brought up in, the very home in which his parents still resided. This weighed heavily on his mind. He asked Marilyn and Linda to sift through all the obituaries and other information they had, hoping they would come across something they may have overlooked.

Ted Rabouin today, with the gun.

ELEVEN

By the time they reached Dave and Linda's house they were all too tired to enjoy the pastry they had purchased earlier. The only thing Marilyn could think of was the warmth of her comfortable bed. Randy was thoroughly exhausted from his tense encounter with Teddy Rabouin. They decided to call it a night. Bidding their farewells to Dave and Linda, Marilyn and Randy headed for the car and began the short drive home.

As soon as they approached their driveway the security light beamed across the front lawn. Randy parked the car and then they both got out and walked the short distance to the door.

"Thank God we installed that light," Marilyn said. "We would still be fumbling around in the dark trying to find the lock."

They both went through their normal routines before retiring. But this particular night was going to be far from normal – it would indeed be a night they would never forget!

Randy was having his second wind and he felt like he needed to unwind. He asked Marilyn to bring him a cup of tea and sit with him in the dining room.

"Aren't you tired?" she asked.

"No, I would just like you to be with me awhile."

He seemed unusually quiet and she could see he was disturbed about something.

When she joined him at the table, he lit a single white candle, one that had been blessed. She could smell the scent as the honeyed wax began to melt.

Mystically the room seemed to take on a strange aura, setting the stage for a most unimaginable phenomenon.

Marilyn watched her husband slump back in the hard maple captain's chair.

"Randy, are you okay?"

He didn't answer.

She felt terrified. Seconds later, he began mumbling something about the past, but she couldn't make out what he was trying to say. Feelings of panic now rushed through her. Jumping to her feet, she reached her arms out, placed her hands on his shoulders and began to shake him, only to find a stranger next to her, a man she had never seen before.

His eyes were filled with rage, his voice deep and distant when he finally answered her question.

"You ask if I am okay, do you?"

Marilyn felt she was in a dangerous situation. If she could only get to the phone to call Dave and Linda!

Fearful of making any sudden moves, knowing her only hope was to stay calm and keep her wits about her, she carefully stepped back away from this stranger.

His eyes were glaring at her as if she had committed some heinous crime. He followed her every move, not letting her out of his sight.

Oh, God, she thought to herself, who could this be? Then she remembered Teddy's words ... "Be prepared, the spirits are going to make lots of trouble for you." This had to be what Teddy was trying to warn them about. He must have recognized that the spirits would come through Randy. He had to be a medium for ... oh, it couldn't be ... for William Prouty. What could she do? She would pray. Teddy told them to pray. She began talking faster than she could think. She found herself in a state of panic, all alone to experience this transfiguration.

"Oh, God, help us! Please don't let any evil come into this house. Please keep us safe from harm. I believe in You ... please help us, heavenly Father. And deliver us from evil, amen!"

Now she had to convince this man, whom she feared was William Prouty, that she was not Maria! How would she accomplish this?

"Oh, God, listen to me," she prayed aloud. "I think I've gone mad! No one will ever believe this ... what is happening to us? Help us get through this night."

She was hoping that what she was about to do would be the right thing. An error here could spell disaster. First, she would try to question him. Maybe he would think she was Chief McKenna!

Her voice trembling, she asked the spirit, "Are you William Prouty?"

"I'm Maria's husband!" he replied sternly.

"What year is it?" she asked.

"Eighteen ninety-nine," he said arrogantly.

Marilyn's heart was pounding as she tried desperately to keep herself under control. There were many questions running through her head. She wanted to know about Maria's death, but she didn't want to send him into a rage. She began searching for the right words.

"Do you know why Maria committed suicide?"

She watched his body stiffen, expecting him to explode with anger at any moment. She prayed he would not harm her.

Instead he broke down and with tear-filled eyes told her, "You know as well as I do, that it was not suicide. I'm here to try and make peace with myself. Enough of these questions! You know the truth about my life ... it's time that you get on with your own lives. Be done with this!"

He lowered his head and began to slip into a calm, serene state.

Marilyn was speechless. She had all she could do to put this whole scene into some kind of rational perspective.

Suddenly the Proutys and Hammonds weren't important. Her concern was now for the present moment. She just wanted their lives together to return to normal. She had to help her husband out of his possessed state.

Standing at arm's length she gently pressed her fingertips against Randy's arm, still fearful of what his reaction might be.

"Randy, can you see me?" she gently asked him.

No answer. Instead he began to weep.

Marilyn was now deeply concerned for him. How did this get so out of hand? And who would ever believe her? How could she ever convince anyone that this bizarre episode had actually taken place when she had a hard time accepting it herself.

Randy lifted his head from its bowed position, where just seconds before he had been weeping. Seeing the concern on Marilyn's face he asked, "What's wrong? I told you I am not tired ... I just want to unwind."

It was apparent to her that Randy had no conception of real-time events. He was carrying on where he had left off before.

"Randy, don't you realize what just happened?"

"What the hell are you talking about, Marilyn?" He was puzzled.

If he couldn't remember what had occurred, then she was the only one left who could.

After she revealed to him the preternatural events and had convinced him how frightened she was, they both knew they had a lot to be concerned about. If a spirit could control Randy's thoughts and actions tonight, it could happen again tomorrow. What they feared was that William had become violent to the point of murdering Maria. If they didn't heed his warning to cease their prying into his past, he might take his fury out on them.

They both fought off sleep that night, afraid of what might happen to them in an unconscious state. But the unavoidable did happen.

After a few fitful attempts at falling asleep, Marilyn fell into a deep slumber. Drifting into a vast valley of fog, she could hear her inner voice talking out loud in her head.

"It's the same moon," the voice began to tell her, " ... not just the phase or month. There is something very special about it, something astrological. It makes it the same as it was back then."

As she tried to make sense of what the voice was telling her, the images of two women appeared in her dream. She watched them as if they were actors on a stage, hearing their every word, seeing their every move. One woman was young; the other much older but not elderly. They were not mother and daughter. The older one had deep-set eyes that showed much sadness, almost depression, but without the tears. They were being compelled by circumstance to do something they had no choice in, and it bothered them to their very souls.

Marilyn's strongest mental impression was of the older woman –clearly she was the more stalwart and determined, unbending in her decisions. The younger woman seemed filled with doubt but did not openly express it.

There was a letter the older woman had written. This she placed in an envelope and sealed it with hot wax which the younger women had melted from a candle. The older woman sat rocking back and forth in a maple rocking chair, clutching a small wooden box in the crook of one arm. She brought it up to her cheek several times and stroked it gently. It was hinged and made of fine-grain hardwood, but it didn't appear to be an heirloom.

When the wax seal had cooled, the younger woman placed the letter inside the box and returned it to the older woman. There was no lock on the box, only a clasp which was tied with a decorative red ribbon. It seemed to have some kind of sentimental value for the older woman, but Marilyn wasn't sure if this value lay in the box itself or in the letter kept inside it. It did seem to comfort the older woman, though.

Then the older woman asked to be helped to the attic. The younger woman complied with her request.

Marilyn watched as they both climbed the stairs to the familiar surroundings of the dungeon-like attic. She then watched them conceal the wooden box under an old blanket which was stored in a corner of the room.

Marilyn knew these women had to be Maria Prouty and her devoted maid, Mary. She surmised that the box contained something of great value. To Maria it was logical, to Marilyn it was not. She wondered why Maria had taken the time to seal the letter and stow it away so carefully. Maria, she thought, must have had great faith in her maid to bestow such confidence in her, to entrust her with certain secrets that created a sacred trust between the two women. Marilyn felt the letter contained answers to Maria's hidden past, answers that she sought to know.

Without warning her dream swept her out of the Prouty mansion and off into the landscape of a field overgrown with weeds and tall grass. Hiding behind two old oak trees was a house – it was the same house in the painting her grandmother had left her. There was a man coming out the door. He was wearing what appeared to be a brown shirt and a pair of brown trousers, but the actual color was darker than tan and lighter than brown, a shade of color which seemed unusual for that time period. She could tell he was a working man and not a man of great wealth. He had been in the house but no one had been at home, and she knew he hadn't stayed long and hadn't touched anything. She sensed that he was linked to all that had been going on and that he must have had a blood connection to the people who owned the house. The style and color of his clothing kept bothering Marilyn – he seemed out of place. Suddenly it dawned on her. What he was wearing was a uniform, the uniform of a Pinkerton detective! He was standing on the pathway in front of the house on Adams Street, the same house in which the gun had been hidden. And he himself was only a player, a custodial and historical link.

Marilyn awakened, her mind still confused by the visions she had while in her dream state. She managed to turn her attention to her husband who was lying next to her.

The events of the night before had also taken their toll on Randy. She noticed that the covers were tossed down to the foot of the bed. It was obvious that he too was having unsettling nightmares which must have been brought on by the extraordinary events of the evening before. She tried to wake him.

"Randy! Randy! Can you hear me?"

He mumbled something but it was hard to make sense of what he was trying to say.

"Come on, Randy, wake up," she begged him.

"Oh, God, Marilyn ... I'm so tired. I had an awful night."

She rubbed his shoulders for a minute, trying to soothe him.

"I dreamed about this damn story, only it didn't seem like a dream ... it was so detailed ... so real!"

She knew just what he meant.

"Randy, let's talk about this over breakfast."

She hurried off to the kitchen. By the time she had toasted the English muffins and poured the steaming hot coffee, Randy was already seated at the table. As he scratched the skin of his receding hairline, Marilyn couldn't help notice how tired he looked. His tan complexion had turned pale and the furrows of his frown lines seemed deeper.

"What weird dreams I had through the night," he told her. "I felt like I was traveling back through time."

Marilyn listened and didn't say a word as Randy told her of the vivid images in his dream.

"I was looking through one of the windows of the Hammond mansion and I could see Henry's body lying on the floor. A man then stooped down near his feet. I know the man was Doctor Norwood because he was carrying a black medical bag. He looked around to see if there were any witnesses before he stuffed a revolver inside his bag. When he glanced up, he saw me. I will never forget the way he looked at me ... the fear I felt when my eyes met his. God, his stare was so intense!"

Randy hesitated for a moment and then continued.

"Suddenly the room filled with darkness and everything I was seeing just vanished. Before I realized it, I found myself standing in a field where an elderly man, with a sickle in his hand, was cutting the tall grass. He must have been a farm hand. He was dressed in black pants and white shirt. He had a long white beard and his face was wizened with age. Cautiously I walked toward him. To my amazement the gentleman began to speak to me, asking if I needed some help. I looked around me to be sure it was me he was talking to. Stuttering, I asked him, 'Is this the Adams farm?' He told me that it was and then wanted to know who I was. Before I could answer him, I wondered what time frame I was in ... was it before or after Henry Hammond's death?"

Randy paused for a moment to catch his breath.

"Then, without thinking, I asked him, 'Do you know who Henry Hammond is?'

'Of course,' he said, 'everyone in town knows who the Hammonds are. You must be a stranger to these parts.'

"Not thinking about what the consequences might be, I said, 'Yes, I am. I wonder if you could tell me if Henry is still alive?'

"This really angered the old man. He began screaming at me, 'Get the hell out of here! Are you crazy or something, asking things like that?'

"He picked up the sickle and began chasing me like a madman. I ran from the field and hid behind a barn down the street, where I watched him. Although I knew I was in another time in history, I knew exactly where I was. There was the old familiar fishing hole, Muzzy Meadows, at the bottom of Adams and Clark streets. I followed him to see what he was up to. The man began to walk towards town, down Adam Street, to Chestnut, up Mechanic, to Wall Street. I figured he must be on his way to Hammond's cold storage plant. Sure enough he lead me right there. In big bold letters atop the double wooden doors was a sign which read 'HAMMOND'S COLD STORAGE.' Unbelievable, I thought."

Marilyn's interest was now at its peak. She shifted her position and continued to listen to his description of the dream. She was fascinated by it all. Randy looked into her eyes and continued.

"I looked around the town and saw the old blacksmith shop and the huge Prouty Boot Company located in the center of town. I even looked inside the windows of the leather goods store on Main Street before I continued on to Jennie Mendell's dress shop. Above that shop was Judge Hill's court house. As I stood there I was amazed to see the judge himself walk out, a giant of a man with a long gray beard and a stern face that appeared to have never cracked a smile. Trying to conceal myself from view, I watched the judge turn the corner off Main Street onto Wall Street. I took a different direction, going down Elm Street, cutting along the railroad track, taking in the rare sight of the old trains as I passed it by. I was totally captivated by everything I saw. Getting as close as I could to listen to what the farm hand had to tell the men inside the plant was not easy. The large windows on the second floor were opened. There were several men inside. One I recognized as Henry ... I remembered the sketch I had previously seen. They took turns looking out the window, as if watching for someone. Suddenly, out of nowhere, another man appeared. I thought I was looking in a mirror ... the man looked like me! ... a little older, but nonetheless the features were the same."

Randy now shifted his gaze toward the wall and continued.

"At that moment the farm hand appeared in the window, shoving his arm as he pointed towards me, yelling, 'There he is ... the man I've been telling you about!' I began to run. The next thing I remember was your shaking me, trying to wake me up. Marilyn, the one thing that made a lasting impression on me was the man who looked just like me! You and Linda have to find more pictures of both families ... I have to know what they look like."

"We'll get them somehow, Randy ... I promise you that," Marilyn told him with genuine assurance.

After Randy finished discussing the details of his dream, Marilyn thought back to hers, wondering about the box that Maria and the maid had taken to the attic. Could Maria be trying to send a message from beyond? She thought back to the day of her tour of Ashcroft and how Eleanor hadn't stored anything in the attic. Marilyn found that to be very strange. If the box did exist, someone knew its contents and its secrets. Could it be Eleanor? How would she ever know, she wondered.

Marilyn knew it wouldn't be easy to continue their search. She was scared, and after last night, she was tempted to quit but something kept urging her on. She knew that when she explained the horrible events she and Randy had experienced the night before to Linda and Dave, Linda especially would be very upset. Linda was already having second thoughts about pursuing the story. She had expressed on many occasions that she was getting very uncomfortable with what had been happening and was thinking about backing off. Marilyn knew Dave would be in favor of his wife's decision if she chose to cease the investigation. Dave wouldn't let himself or his wife get caught up with the unexplainable, even if it were staring him in the face.

After a long discussion and a lot of pleading with Linda later that morning, Marilyn convinced her friend to stay on.

That afternoon they returned to the Richard Sugden Library and, once inside, descended the stairs to its local history museum. They frantically looked for pictures, sketches or photographs of the Proutys and Hammonds. They poured through page after page in all the scrapbooks that contained photographs and sketches of other Prouty and Hammond descendants. However, photographs of Maria and the other key characters were nowhere to be found. It was obvious that their photographs had been deliberately taken from the yellowed pages of the scrapbooks. Only their names remained under blank spaces where the photos should have been mounted, proving that they had indeed once existed, but for some strange reason they had now mysteriously disappeared.

All Marilyn and Linda had now were the sketches. Both wondered why someone would go to such extremes to remove photographs from the museum's scrapbooks. It struck them as an odd thing to do.

"We have to find a way," Linda told Marilyn. "Someone must have photos of these people!"

Linda thought again for a moment. "I know who might have a lot of memorabilia ... Dave's cousin, Christine. I'm going to call her this afternoon. If she can't get her hands on photos of the Proutys and Hammonds, I bet she can at least get us some photos of Spencer, showing us the way the town looked back in eighteen ninety-nine. This way we can see how accurate Randy's dream was."

Linda continued.

"Oh, one more thing ... I know someone else who might be able to help us obtain photographs of the two families ... her name is Frances. She is an acquaintance of mine. Frances will know where to find the photos we're looking for, and maybe at the same time she can give us some insight into the story."

Marilyn looked puzzled. "How can you be so sure?"

"Frances has psychic abilities."

Marilyn looked at her with surprise. "Why didn't you mention her before?"

"I was afraid ... I didn't really believe in people who claimed they had psychic powers. But ever since we visited Teddy ... well, let's just say it's changed my perception of things."

"Then let's go for it!" Marilyn replied excitedly.

Linda called Christine right away. She was happy to help out. Without much delay she was able to locate a bicentennial book that featured photographs of the town as it looked in the 1800s. She delivered it to Linda's house early that same evening. And again, wasting no time, a meeting with Frances was also arranged for the following night.

While on their way to Worcester, Marilyn and Linda decided that they would give Frances the same information about the gun as they had given to Teddy, guarding it as if it were the ultimate possession in their lives and revealing only what was necessary. In their opinion, the less Frances knew, the more credible she would be if she came up with the facts as they knew them.

Their experience with Frances was not as dramatic as it had been with Teddy. She lived in a small ranch house off June Street in Worcester. Her home blended in with all the familiar surroundings that one would see on any given day in urban America – there were children playing in the living room, and coming from one of the bedrooms down the hall was music only a teenager could appreciate.

Frances asked them to follow her to a small room just off to the right of the kitchen. A small wooden gate stretched across the entrance, preventing a large black labrador retriever from approaching them. The dog was whimpering and wagging its tail, trying to get Frances's attention. As they entered the room she closed the door behind them, telling them that she didn't want her children to hear what they were about to discuss.

The room looked like it was used for a small office, but there was no desk. Instead there were a few chairs, a small round table and a day-bed. She asked them to be seated. Frances sat directly across from Linda, settling her petit body back against the chair and placing her legs up under her, Indian style. Her long brown hair brushed down across her shoulders.

Linda took the initiative. She removed the gun from her bag and handed it to the woman. Frances held the gun for a moment, leaned forward and placed it against her forehead. Instantly she shifted her position and sat up straight in the chair, staring wide-eyed at Linda. Frances mumbled something but it didn't make sense to either of them. She closed her eyes once again and the room filled with a dead silence. It seemed like an eternity before Frances finally spoke.

She told Linda and Marilyn that the gun was used in a terrible crime, not to kill one person, but two.

"A woman was connected to this weapon, but she was not slain with it. However, there was foul play ... strangulation at the hands of her husband. I can't come up with any names, but I feel this happened in the 1800s. I see horse-drawn carriages and Victorian clothing ... I also feel a presence among us which I can't describe. That's all I can tell you."

Frances didn't spend as much time with them as Teddy had, nor did she go into as many details. But she did give Marilyn and Linda what they were hoping for, and in return they gave her more clues as to what they were doing.

The following afternoon Frances surprised them with an unexpected telephone call.

"The story kept bothering me," she explained. "I hope you don't mind, but I took it upon myself to go to the Worcester Public Library and do some research of my own."

She asked if one of them would like to pick up the information she had obtained. Dave, who was listening in on the office phone, volunteered to go over and get the paperwork before she left for work.

When Dave arrived Frances asked him to come in. She led him to the small room where she, Linda and Marilyn had talked the night before. The door was closed, and when she opened it, the foul odor that emanated from the room was enough to make Dave sick – it was like nothing he had ever smelled before.

"The only explanation for that terrible smell," Frances explained, "is probably due to the presence I felt in the room last night. The windows have been opened all day and the horrid odor is still there."

Shaking his head in disbelief Dave picked up the paperwork, wished Frances well and hurried out the door. When he arrived home, Randy and Marilyn were there waiting in the kitchen with Linda. He didn't have to say a thing – they knew by his expression that something was wrong. He sat down in one of the kitchen chairs, his olfactory senses still overtaken by the acrid odor. He tried to explain what had happened.

"The only way I can describe it ... it was like a thousand rats had died and then rotted for months."

"Could the odor have been manmade?" Marilyn asked him.

"Marilyn, I don't know of anything that smells that bad or could linger that long. Besides, who in their right mind would introduce such an awful odor into their home?"

The following day they had another surprise from Frances. She called Linda and explained that she had gone back to the Worcester Public Library and had managed to obtain some pictures which the four of them would find most interesting. This is what they had been searching for all along! The paperwork she had given Dave the day before contained information they already had – the pictures were what they needed.

That same day Frances delivered the photos to Dave and Linda's home where all four were impatiently waiting. As she entered the kitchen, Randy was the first to speak. He expressed how nervous he was about viewing the photos.

As he spoke, Frances turned her attention abruptly toward him. She brought her hand up to her chest, as if in pain, and gasped, "Oh, my God! I can see why you have such an interest in finding out the truth behind the deaths. The story is about your family ... isn't it?"

Before Randy could say anything, she continued. "I can see the resemblance. It's uncanny how much you look like him!"

Randy was shaking his head in denial while the others looked on.

"It's not my family," he replied, apparently irritated.

Frances stared at them. She could see that none of them were prepared for this.

Marilyn reached for the pictures, anxious to find out what she meant by her statement. They gathered around so they could all view the photos. To

189

their surprise they were photographs of sketches, but at least Frances had managed to get all of them. And at the top of the small pile was Aaron Hammond himself!

"This is the man I saw in my dream!" Randy shouted. You could hear a pin drop.

Linda felt the fear rush through her body. What stared back at her so hauntingly was a sketch of a man that could have been Randy himself.

Frances interrupted their thoughts.

"I hate to tell you this, but I get the feeling that the four of you are connected to these people. You have been brought together for a reason ... it's possible that you could have been the murder victims. Do you believe in reincarnation?"

No one answered.

Frances went on to explain her views about past lives. She could see that Randy, Dave and Linda were uncomfortable with what she was telling them. Marilyn, however, was deeply interested in what she was trying to explain about past life regression.

"It's odd that you should bring this subject up," Marilyn said. "For the past few months I've had this same idea in my mind. I can sort of place all of us."

"Don't be silly, Marilyn," Linda interrupted. "Your imagination is running away with you."

"No ... you're wrong, Linda. You've talked about reincarnation yourself ... admit it." Linda nodded.

"Please hear me out," she begged.

"Go on, Marilyn, I'm interested in what you have to say," Frances interjected.

Dave and Randy were quiet. Looking at each other, they shrugged their shoulders, wondering what flashes of intuition Marilyn would unveil.

"This is how I see it, Randy. Obviously it's Aaron ... everything indicates that fact, except for that one night in particular when we had that strange experience after visiting Teddy."

Frances didn't ask her to explain what she meant by that statement. Instead she was intent on hearing what Marilyn was leading up to.

"As for Dave, he believes there's a logical explanation for everything. The facts are what he's after, just as William McDonald, the reporter, was a century ago."

Marilyn continued with her past-life theories.

"Linda, however, is the emotional type. Her feelings are hurt very easily, and when they are, she retaliates and presses forward to establish her point. I feel she could have been Maria Prouty since Maria was a very sensitive person. As for me, I'm sure that I was Chief George McKenna. I love investigating things ... I'm inquisitive and I'm always searching for the truth."

Silence fell upon the room as the others stared at each other.

"Marilyn, think about what your saying," Linda replied with an embarrassed look.

"I'm not saying I'm right, but that's exactly what my impression is of who's who."

Frances interrupted, breaking the tension between the two women.

"Marilyn, I think you may be close to the truth. I'm not sure you're totally accurate as to who everyone might have been, but my psychic instincts tell me you're close."

It was hard enough to face the fact that Randy's dream had become reality – the blacksmith shop, the Prouty Boot Company and the other scenes he had described in such detail. Now it was all coming alive through the pages in the bicentennial book Christine had loaned them.

Marilyn continued to sort through the sketches. A picture of Henry and Iris fell from the bottom of the pack onto the table. Their sketched portraits were the same as the ones that had been displayed on the front page of the paper in the early eighties. A sketch of William was under theirs, his eyes boldly staring out from dark, heavy brows. His mustache and nineteenth-century apparel seemed to fit his stern outward appearance. This was the way Teddy had described him minutes before he saw the sketch. Marilyn knew without a doubt that William's spirit that night had willed itself into Randy's soul, his eyes becoming a mirror into William's past.

The last sketch was that of Aaron's love – Maria Prouty, the veiled lady herself, the same woman that had appeared in Linda's nightmares.

AARON HAMMOND

HENRY HAMMOND

IRIS PROUTY

MARIA PROUTY

WILLIAM PROUTY

Her long dark hair was pulled back in a bun. Her deep-set eyes portrayed a certain sadness.

Finally they knew what Aaron and Maria looked like. Could it be possible that Maria's image was what they really saw in the window of the Prouty mansion, or had their imaginations gotten the better of them?

Frances looked at some of their research notes. She was clearly interested in the obituaries. Linda had her briefcase leaning up against the leg of the chair, next to her. Frances seemed to know what she wanted, pulling out Charles Dumas's obituary, silently reading as the others chatted amongst themselves, discussing Albert Nichols's date of death.

Frances looked up from the paperwork.

"Excuse me ... I don't mean to interrupt, but where in Spencer is Upper Wire Village?"

"That's were I was brought up," Randy explained. "My parents still live there. The wire mills used to be located in that part of town until we had the flood sometime in the 1950s."

"Do you know where number two mill house is?" she asked.

Randy was suspicious of the question. He was almost afraid to respond, worried that he was going to be told something he didn't want to hear. His speech failing him, all he could manage was a nod.

"Charles Dumas was murdered there," she said bluntly.

Everyone was silent. The words had a numbing effect, paralyzing their will to ask anything, leaving them to sit there in a state of disbelief. Nothing made sense. Frances handed Marilyn the obituary to confirm the address for herself.

"How did we overlook this?" Dave whispered.

"Teddy said you were brought up in the same house in which one of the murdered victims used to live."

Here was another link in the chain that bonded them together, connecting them to the victim's past.

Frances broke the somber mood that seemed to cast itself over the foursome.

"I heard you mention the name Albert ... something about going to his grave?"

"That's right ... we want to reconfirm his date of death," Linda replied.

"Well, if you would like, I would be very glad to go over to the cemetery with you. I might be able to get some kind of feeling about him ... from his final resting place."

They all looked at each other.

"You know psychics can do strange things!" she said laughing. "I'm only kidding," she added, trying to put the four of them at ease.

"Would you be willing to go to the cemetery now?" Marilyn asked.

"It's eight o'clock!" Linda blurted.

Ignoring Linda, Frances responded to Marilyn's question.

"Why not? We can take a couple of flashlights to help us find Albert's grave."

"We know where it is ... we've been there before," Marilyn exclaimed excitedly.

"Oh, no ... someone will see us for sure!" Linda shouted. "Evergreen Cemetery can be seen from Route 9."

"Lighten up, Linda, you worry too much!" Dave interjected.

Randy laughed, and giving her a little nudge, said, "Come on, we can all pile into the station wagon."

After the short ride from Spencer to East Brookfield, Randy drove through the opened gates and proceeded a few yards down the narrow roadway into Evergreen Cemetery. The headlights from the car shined on the tombstones, making the light from the high beams dance out from the blackness of the night. Randy drew a deep breath as he brought the car to a full stop.

"The grave is right there ... the second row in," Randy said as he pointed it out to the rest.

They emerged from the car and carefully followed him, tiptoeing through the rows, like one would tiptoe through a sleeping person's bedroom. Frances reached her hands out, touching the stone as the others watched in silence.

"Aaron Hammond was the cause of Albert Nichols's death," Frances explained. "He and some judge had signed many fraudulent documents together. Albert knew too much and had to be taken care of."

Frances related this in a positive manner, just as Teddy had.

Randy, a bit shaken by what was happening, stepped to the side, trying to clear his mind. Leaning his chin into the palm of his hand, his eyes drifted to another headstone which bore the name "Nichols." He knelt down to get a closer look. He held onto the monument to balance himself. Suddenly he felt a surge of electricity pulsate through his body as he heard a desperate voice scream out, "My son was murdered! He was murdered! Help his soul rest ... you know the truth!"

Randy quickly pulled his arm away, then stumbled and lost his balance. Dave grabbed him.

"Hey, what's the matter, Randy? Are you okay?"

"Didn't you hear that awful screaming about her son's murder?"

"What are you talking about, buddy?" Dave asked him.

"He needs to rest," Frances broke in. "Clearly he has some psychic abilities, but I don't think he should be using them."

Randy tried to explain how he had touched the stone just to maintain his balance. Then he realized it was Albert's mother's headstone when her screams echoed inside his head.

Dave took the keys from his friend.

"I'll drive home," he said.

After they reached their destination, Frances motioned for them to sit down around the kitchen table.

"Look, I would like to give you all some advice," Frances began. "Take it for what it's worth. You are dealing with the unknown ... this story is full of evil. It is my personal belief that you have all the information you need to write your book. I know you want to find out about Iris, but I feel you should make that your last attempt before something happens."

TWELVE

They knew Frances was right. They should stop while they could, but with Marilyn and Linda's growing belief in past life regression they felt they should pursue the one last avenue that was available to them. They remembered that John, the photographer, knew someone who had studied past life regressions. After much deliberation they set up an appointment with him for the following evening.

After getting the information they needed from John, the four of them headed for the beautiful colonial town of Sturbridge, Massachusetts, following the directions he had given them.

Finally they arrived in front of a very modest home. Two young men greeted them. They seemed pleasant enough. While the introductions were being made, Linda glanced over at Marilyn, watching her friend's eyes scan the room in her usual observant manner. Just like McKenna would have done, she thought to herself.

Suddenly, Linda spotted what had caught Marilyn's eye. The wooden molding just above the door casing was heavily accented with purple paint. At first, Linda didn't understand the reason for such poor taste, but then she realized the meaning behind it. This was symbolic of devil worship. Was she right in thinking these two young men could be part of a cult? John said that they dealt with past life regressions. Could there be more to it?

While Linda was analyzing the scene, the two young men invited her and the others to be seated in the living room. A round table sat in the middle of the room, a ouija board placed in the center, and adjacent to it a lap-top computer. This was not what they had expected.

Linda's mental deliberations came to an abrupt end when the two young men, who had introduced themselves as Steve and Tim, placed their hands on the triangular piece of plastic. They moved it about with their long, sleek fingers, gliding the object over the board like it was some form of art. Their hands seemed to float faster and faster over the letters displayed boldly in black. Then, without warning, the name "Phil" was spelled out on the board.

Dave's eyes widened with disbelief when he saw it. The young men looked towards them.

"Who's Phil?" Steve asked. Dave struggled with his reply.

"Phil was my father ... he died a few years ago," he finally managed to answer. "There is no way that this can be my dad! How did you come up with that name?"

The two men moved their hands away from the board. Tim began typing into the computer everything that was being said, while Steve responded to Dave's sudden outburst with a calm tone, asking him if he would like to ask the spirit a question.

All eyes were on Dave as he gruffly agreed to do so. He made it clear that he did not believe in what they were doing. He just wanted to get through the evening's charade and get on with reality.

After regaining his composure and feeling somewhat awkward, Dave asked, "Dad, is that you?"

Steve's and Tim's hands once again seemed to be guided back and forth over the letters on the ouija board. The letters soon spelled out words put in the form of a question, and this gave Dave a nearly heart-stopping shock.

"WHO DO YOU THINK IT IS? ... SANTA CLAUS?"

"My father used to say that when he joked around with me," Dave cried in amazement. "How can this be possible?"

Before Dave or the others had a chance to deal with their emotions, Steve and Tim received another message from the spirit, a message so frightening that they all insisted the two men stop at once. The cold, harsh words screamed out a warning from beyond ...

"DESTROY THE GUN OR IT WILL KILL AGAIN. YOU MUST FILL

THE BARREL WITH LEAD AND BURY IT IN THE GROUND!"

Dave suddenly pushed his chair away from the table and stood up.

"I don't want to hear any more of this!" he screamed.

It was obvious that his wife and friends felt the same way. They were very uncomfortable with the whole thing, concluding it was best to leave.

It was at that point the four reached a decision. Without a doubt they knew now that they had to disassociate themselves from psychics, past life regressions and, most definitely, ouija boards. It was against everything they were taught to believe in.

After the strange evening ended, Dave welcomed the quiet solitude of the night. His mind slipped into a peaceful place – not sleep, but a deep tranquil rest. And here Frances appeared to him.

In his near dream-like state, Frances stressed that he was the most logical one of the four, and that he had to warn the others, as she had, to bring the search to an end. Her words echoed in his head as he lay there, trying to make sense of all that had happened.

Reflecting on this, he recalled the inexplicable events that occurred when Linda and Marilyn were in the beginning stages of piecing the story together. He remembered the light switch in the kitchen and how it crackled and smoked only when Linda touched it. And then he recalled that the lights would go out when she sat down to write. It had reached the point where they had no choice but to call an electrician. After searching every junction box and following wire after wire, he was unable to come up with a solution.

But then it all seemed to stop on its own.

Dave then reflected on how Marilyn experienced a similar problem. Several times her computer screen displayed letters and numbers all jumbled together, although she had never hit so much as one key on the keyboard. It was all so bizarre.

What was the meaning behind this mystery? Would they ever really know, or would it remain unsolved? Dave knew it was time to put everything together and bring the story to an end, if that were possible.

THIRTEEN

The story with all its bizarre twist and turns had to be told. Maybe then they could get on with their lives. To do this they had to find out about the one person who suffered the worst loss of all – Iris Prouty. Their intense search showed that she had purposely left an untraceable path, but this did not deter them. They had run into a lot of closed doors while searching for answers, yet they still pressed on.

They finally traced where Iris had lived during the final days of her earthly sojourn. It was through an obituary of her late husband, Wesley A. O'Leary, whom she had married later in life, that they had resided in Hillside, New Jersey. He had passed away on 2 January 1937, the same month as Henry Hammond, thirty-eight years later.

O'Leary's obituary, however, didn't indicate where in Hillside he was buried. It was obvious Iris had gone to great lengths to keep their lives a secret, even in death.

With a little checking, they discovered that the Higgins and Bonner Funeral Home had taken care of Mr. O'Leary's funeral arrangements. Marilyn called them to see what information she could obtain. They learned that O'Leary had been cremated at the Rose Hill Crematory in Linden, New Jersey. His ashes had been retrieved by an unknown family member who returned them to Massachusetts, but the director of the funeral home didn't know to which town or city they were taken. Marilyn thought that Iris must have made the arrangements, after all she was his wife.

Through an undisclosed source, they learned that O'Leary had been born and brought up in Southboro, Massachusetts, a Metro West suburb. On a hunch they decided to take a chance and explore Southboro's two cemeteries.

Their first stop was the Rural Cemetery, and unlike their previous visits to cemeteries, this time they didn't hesitate to check in with the office. They had been through too much and come too far to worry about what people thought of their investigation.

After they had entered the small stone building, the young lady, who was sitting behind the office desk, got up and approached them.

"Hello, may I help you?" she asked them cordially.

After they explained their purpose for being there, she stepped back away from them. She had a look of suspicion on her face.

"Look, I know our request sounds strange, but please let me explain," Randy told her. "My friends and I are writing a book, and this information we're asking for is extremely important to our story. If we were to find Mr. O'Leary's grave, this would lead us to his wife, Iris, who would surely be buried beside him."

Instantly the corners of her mouth turned up into a smile. With the palm of her hand she swept her long curly brown hair off her shoulders and proudly introduced herself as Bridget, asking that her name be used in the book. Randy nodded in the affirmative.

With that she pivoted her body around.

"Follow me, please," she told them. She went straight to the record cabinets to search for the documents.

After a few minutes she announced, "Here it is! This is where Mr. O"Leary's plot is located."

"What about Iris, his wife? ... is she buried here also?"

"Let me check."

The anxiety was more than they could stand. After all their efforts they silently prayed they would find Iris.

"Yes, she is buried right next to her husband. I have the document right here. She died on October 12, 1967. She was eighty-seven years old."

"Oh, God ... finally we've come to the end of our search," Marilyn said with a sigh of relief.

"I'll be glad to walk you over to the area. I know right where it is."

"Thank you," replied Randy. "We would appreciate that very much,"

It was hard to believe that after eighteen months they were finally getting somewhere.

As Bridget led them through the winding pathway, Randy tried to get his wife's and friends' attention without it being obvious to Bridget. He pointed to the sky and they knew immediately what he meant. Since they first began their search, this was the only time they had walked through a cemetery without a drop of rain falling on them. Maybe it was really over.

"Here we are ... this is Mr. O'Leary's gravesite."

To their surprise, only a single name was inscribed on the headstone, that of "Wesley A. O'Leary."

"I thought you said Iris was buried here," Marilyn said.

The young lady looked just as shocked as they did. She still had the document in her hand. She looked at it once again, her eyes scanning it closely.

"The paper states that she was cremated at the Ewing Crematory in Trenton, New Jersey. Her funeral service was at the Kimball Funeral Home in Princeton. She prearranged her own funeral through the Princeton Bank and Trust. She is definitely buried here right next to her husband. I know it's unusual not to have both names inscribed on the marker, but I'm sure it was at Mrs. Prouty-O'Leary's request."

After a few minutes of silence they thanked Bridget for her help. She wished them luck with their book and then headed back to the cemetery office.

They remained behind for a brief period of time, consumed with how Iris's secrets were carried with her, deep within the soil that now blanketed her grave. She didn't want to leave any traces of the terrible truth behind. This was the only way it could end for her.

Linda felt an emptiness deep within. She turned and walked a short distance away from the others. Feeling mixed emotions she gazed across the cemetery.

Now alone with her own thoughts, she heard what sounded like a faint whisper. It was the same low tone she heard when she first sat down in her study to read about the mystery. She looked in the direction she thought the sound was coming from. In the distance she could see the silhouette of a woman standing behind a large pine tree. The woman's hair was pulled back in a bun and she was dressed in Victorian-style clothing.

Linda couldn't see her face clearly. The sun was streaming down, casting a bright light over her body. Linda hurried toward her, but as she got closer, the woman vanished. She stood there looking all around, but there was nothing that remotely resembled what she saw. She couldn't bring herself to tell the others, and besides what good would it do? The four of them had been through this kind of experience before. Maybe her imagination was simply playing tricks on her.

This was the final link in the chain that would lock away forever a small town's chilling secrets of the past.

CONCLUSION

The coincidence of finding the gun, having a painting of the house it was hidden in, just as it appeared back in the 1800s, and the fact that one of us was brought up in the home of one murder victim, was not left to chance. As strange as it may sound, there had to be a guiding force that put the four of us together, allowing us each to have a piece of a very complicated puzzle to work with in order to turn the lies of suicide into the facts of murder. We feel that Maria's spirit was our guide.

Through our research into the Prouty-Hammond tragedies we have concluded that Iris Prouty was Henry Hammond's only true love. He visited her only hours before his death, carrying with him the burden of a secret message that had been delivered to him by his good friend, Albert Nichols. Their passion and undying love for each other may have resulted in Iris becoming pregnant, and this could explain the articles we found on the headstones of Henry's and Maria's graves. It is possible that one of their descendants placed them on the headstones, but we will never know for sure.

We then had to try to piece together the details of the mystery. What follows is the result of that effort.

Aaron's sin came back to haunt him in a way he had never expected when the veiled mystery lady herself, Maria Prouty, secretly arranged to meet with him in a wooded area outside of town, months before the wedding. She told him that the marriage had to be stopped, confessing that Iris was his daughter, and that she was the results of thier past affair. He had worked too hard and come too far to let this ruin his good name. The wedding wouldn't take place no matter what the cost, even if it meant murder. He would see to that. Aaron thought out his plan carefully and relied on the many connections he had in town.

Rumors circulated that he had dealt with some questionable business situations, including illegal beef shipments to areas of the country as far away as Colorado. Aaron used the services of the Pinkerton railway detective agency on many occasions, so it didn't look peculiar to anyone when he was notified by the agency that Berry's body had been found and that he personally arranged for the shipment of the body back to Jason Adams's house. It was in this house that the gun was found seventy-two years later.

With the power Hammond had, he could have easily arranged for Frank Berry to be eliminated. Unfortunately, Taylor and Dumas met with the same fate as their friend Berry, which all led back to Hammond.

Aaron Hammond had planned well in advance. If you read the facsimiles of the funeral ledgers in the appendix, you will notice that a very inexpensive casket was purchased anonymously through Henry's estate on 21 October 1898, two and a half months before Henry's wedding. Why would a young man who was planning for a future with his bride to be order a casket? If you scan down the pages of the ledger a little further, you will also notice that, after Henry's death, another casket was purchased by Aaron Hammond, a very expensive one. The purchase of the first casket two and a half months prior might put a thought in people's minds that Henry had been planning to commit suicide all along, erasing the fact that it could very well have been murder. This was the plan that Aaron Hammond devised.

Chief McKenna was the last one to be called to the murder scenes where the two wealthy families, as well as Dumas, were involved. Dr. Norwood, a good friend to both Hammond and Prouty, was summoned to the houses first and ruled each death a suicide. If Henry Hammond and Charles Dumas did commit suicide, why did the gun mysteriously disappear? How did the gun get to the North Adams Street house? We feel Dr. Norwood, along with Jason Adams, may have put it there. They were all close friends who had a lot of financial ties to each other and the town.

Every Friday, in the chilling month of January, at the stroke of 6:00 a.m., the angel of death knocked on Spencer's door to take another soul connected to the Prouty-Hammond mystery. A seed of evil grew out of the hidden affair between Aaron Hammond and Maria Prouty, and it followed them, eventually destroying their lives with guilt and remorse.

Aaron Hammond died on 22 November 1911. He had gone to the stable to check on his horses. When he didn't return to the house, his clerk, Martin McCarthy, who was living at the Hammond estate, went to the barn and found Aaron lying on the hay-covered floor. Martin immediately called Dr. Norwood. The medical examiner reported that Hammond had died of heart disease. Like the others, the angel of death claimed his soul at the appointed hour: 6:00 a.m.

Through our research we discovered that some of the information in the articles we read was incorrect. Maria Prouty died thirty-six hours after Henry Hammond. George Dumas's real name was Charles Demers, just as Teddy Rabouin had said. The death certificate we found attests to that fact.

We also believe that some of the facts were altered to sensationalize the 1941 article about the Prouty and Hammond tragedies. We have a strong feeling that the mystery writer was Will McDonald.

Evil never dies and violence keeps a soul from coming to rest. We have tried, to the best of our ability, to come as close as possible to the truth behind the Prouty-Hammond tragedies. We hope that the souls of all the victims will now finally rest in peace.

APPENDIX

Extracts from the *Worcester Telegram*

HIDDEN

MOTIVES

SPENCER SLOW TO YIELD ITS SECRETS.

IRENE PROUTY LEARNS HER MOTHER'S FATE.

SUSPICIONS ABROAD OF

ROPE AND HANGING.

OFFICIALS' MOUTHS TIGHT
TO ALL INQUIRY.

BOSTON SIRIVES TO FERRET AND
TAKES THE ONLY.

COPIES IN FULL TELEGRAM
EXCLUSIVES.

Family Friends Praise Pictorial
Exclusives.

Special to The Telegram

SPENCER, Jan. 9--*As the days go by public interest in the terrible double tragedy loses none of its attraction for the people who feel a desire to know the inmost facts of* the suicides. More closely than ever are both families guarding the secret. Not a person in Spencer believes but a dark motive caused two estimable people to seek death.

The lack of a definite statement, instead of shielding the families from unnecessary publicity, serves only to make the affair more sensational in character and the very mystery attached to the causes of deaths has awakened more widespread curiosity. This interest is perfectly natural, and will continue in force for a long time. Why the real facts of Mrs Prouty's death should be kept a secret is only another of the mysteries surrounding this most mysterious case.

Both the Hammond and Prouty families very naturally shrink from widespread notoriety of the double suicide, and it is to be expected that kind friends should try to spare the sensitive feelings of every person concerned.

That Mrs. Prouty hanged herself in the attic of her home on Ash street, and that a rope was used instead of the silk handkerchief which was on her shoulders when the body was lying on the bed, is the belief of many people in Spencer.

Medical Examiner Dr. E. W. Norwood was seen this afternoon for The Telegram, but refused to discuss the suicide cases. In answer to a question, the doctor replied that he had not yet filed his official report of the deaths with Dist. Atty. Rockwood Hoar. Dr. Norwood is a personal friend of both families, and his reticence is in the interests of the sorrow-stricken kindred.

The sensational report that Henry Hammond was in love with Miss Florence L. Johnson and killed himself through despair because he was about to marry another girl was investigated today by a reporter and found to be untrue. If young Hammond loved Miss Johnson, as rumor had it, the girl never knew it. Miss Johnson was Hammond's first cousin. Her mother and Henry's mother were sisters, daughters of Elliot Swan of Worcester.

Mr. Swan was a long-time resident of Worcester, and owned the old hotel which used to stand where union station in the city is built. The old hotelkeeper died wealthy and bequeathed many thousand dollars to Miss Johnson and her sister. An heiress in her own right, Miss Johnson is the daughter of wealthy parents. Her father, Charles F. Johnson, is in Boulder, Col. this week with his wife and younger daughter.

He is proprietor of one of the largest wholesale meat commission houses in Denver, Col. and in company with a wealthy Chicago lawyer owns several ranches, one of them being a fertile tract of 1000 acres in Texas. Mr. Johnson is a son of Justin D. Johnson of Barre.

Mrs. Aaron Hammond, mother of the dead man, positively said to a Spencer gentleman that there was nothing beyond cousinly regards between her son and her niece. Mrs. Hammond said that Henry's engagement to Miss Iris G. Prouty was brought about by Miss Johnson, who took a cousinly interest in Henry. This authoritative statement disposes of the sentimental theory that Henry shot himself on account of disappointed love. But, although theory after theory is exploded, the double mystery remains as dark as ever.

Nothing but sympathy being expressed for both families.

Miss Iris G. Prouty was made aware of her mother's suicide today. The distracted girl wanted to look upon her kind mother's dead face for the last time, but it was thought best that this should not be so. News of her mother's tragic end was imparted to the agonized girl as carefully as could be, and the blow was an addition to the terrible one which she had already faced. Fields M. Prouty and his wife, uncle and aunt of Miss Prouty told her as gently as possible. How the girl took the news was not made public, but it is said that the great burden of grief is affecting the girl's health.

Miss Louise Prouty, younger daughter of the dead woman, has not been informed of the true cause of her mother's death, and the facts will be shielded from her as long as possible. She arrived from college to attend her mother's funeral which took place this afternoon. Miss Louise was escorted home from college by Mr. Myron A. Young. Mr. Young had the duty to perform of telling the girl of her mother's death. This he did not tell her until they had arrived in sight of the house. Miss Louise bore the news quite bravely, although the death of her mother came to her as a severe shock.

The truth will be mercifully concealed from her, and as soon as her grief will permit, she will return to Wellesley, where associations and study will deaden her sorrow.

But few of the most intimate friends of the Prouty family were present at the funeral this afternoon. The funeral was private. Those who were there were the husband and daughters, William F. Peel of Staffordville, Ct., Walter Peel, Worcester, brothers, Miss Emma Peel, Worcester, a sister, Fields M. Prouty and wife, and Millins W. Prouty. A. E. Kingsley was funeral director. Rev. Sherman W. Brown officiated. The casket was borne by James H. Ames, Noah Sagendorph, Thomas J. Coupin and Myron A. Young. There was no singing. Interment was in Pine Grove cemetery.

Medical examiner Dr. E. W. Norwood's certificate of death and burial permit given to Undertaker A. E. Kingsley, and filed tonight at the town clerk's office, throws no new light upon Mrs. Prouty's death. It gives the cause of death as suicide, but no details.

As the days pass, the mystery gets deeper and deeper. Some of the most astounded theories are afloat and the interest in the case is more intense tonight than ever. News of the double tragedy has drifted to Boston, and tonight two reporters of Boston papers landed in town equipped for business pointers with The Telegram's news articles of this morning. One Boston paper used The Telegram's story verbatim tonight, and gave credit for it, where credit belonged. The pictures used by The Telegram in illustrating the article today were returned this afternoon to the friends of the Hammond and Prouty families, who as kindly loaned them to The Telegram. The pictures in The Telegram were excellent likeness, and reflect great credit upon The Telegram's artist. Other papers used fake pictures, one Worcester morning paper in particular, using photograph of Miss Louise I. Prouty represent her sister, Iris. And the copy was not a good copy of the photograph at that. The friends who courteous loaned genuine pictures to The Telegraph, did so with the understanding the correct copies of the originals be made. The friends were satisfied with the excellent pictures in the paper.

SPENCER'S DOUBLE TRAGEDY

Death of Mrs. Prouty Was a

Great Shock

Sympathy felt for the Afflicted—The
Startling Sequel to the Hammond suicide.

There are no new developments today in the two tragic events at Spencer. The town, shocked by the self-inflicted death of Henry Hammond Friday, was startled again Saturday, night by the news of the death of Mrs. William H. Prouty, the mother of Miss Iris Prouty, Mr. Hammond's fiancee. Mrs. Prouty had been in poor health for some time and was undoubtedly overcome by the tragedy of Friday, which affected her daughter so closely. She took her own life by strangulation Saturday afternoon.

MRS. PROUTY'S DEATH

Supposed to be the results of temporary

mental derangement.

Mrs. Prouty had been alone Saturday afternoon and Mr. Prouty, on return from his office, failing to find her as usual in the lower part of the house, made a search and discovered her in one of the attic chambers, with life extinct, a silk handkerchief twisted around her neck showing the cause of death. The family physician Dr. E. W. Norwood, was hastily summoned, but all efforts to revive her were unavailing.

It is supposed that the act was the results of a fit of temporary mental derangement, brought on by the great shock caused by the death of Henry Hammond, who was to have been married to Mrs. Prouty's daughter, Miss Iris, tomorrow. Mrs. Prouty had been an invalid for a number of years and rarely went into society. No letter announcing to any member of the family her intentions has been discovered. The medical examiner, Dr. Norwood, stated that death had probably resulted an hour before she was found. This second blow falls with crushing weight upon each member of the family. Besides her husband Mrs. Prouty leaves two daughters, Iris and Louise. Miss Iris was at the Hammond residence when the sad news was brought to her by her cousin, Millins W. Prouty. Louise, the second daughter, is attending college at Wellesley, where she was informed of the event. She arrived home yesterday. The family have the deepest sympathy of all the community in their infliction.

Mrs. Prouty was 50 years of age and her maiden name was Maria J. Peel. She was the daughter of Mr. and Mrs. Joseph Peel. She was born in Leicester. Her father went to Spencer in 1866 and started a woolen industry in the mill now run by A. L. Taft. Mr.

Peel removed to Holyoke in 1872, still continuing in the business of manufacturing woolen goods until his death, about 20 years ago. Mrs. Prouty was married to William H. Prouty of the firm of Prouty Bros. 27 years ago. A brother William F. Peel of Staffordville, Ct. and two sisters, Mrs. Ella Condy of Boston and Miss Emma F. Peel of Worcester, also survive. Another sister, who died many years ago, was the wife of Fields M. Prouty, her husband's brother.

The funeral services were held at the house on Ash street this afternoon, and were private. Sherman W. Brown, pastor of the First Congregational church, presided.

The funeral of Henry Hammond was from his father's home at 2 o'clock Sunday afternoon. Miss Iris Prouty was present, although her friends had attempted to dissuade her from undergoing the severe ordeal. She bore her grief bravely, although it was feared that she could break down.

The casket covered with flowers, stood in an upstairs room. The body was clothed in the suit prepared for the wedding, and the white hands were filled with flowers, the gift of Miss Prouty. Rev. Sherman W. Brown, pastor of the First Congregational church, read from the Scriptures and offered prayer. A quartet, composed Miss Florence Muzzy, Mrs. W. H. Hathaway, William A. Haskins and George D. Muzzy, sang "Abide with Me," "Rest, Spirit, Rest," and "Still, Still with Thee." The bearers were Millins W. Prouty and E. Bruce Dunn, who were to have been ushers at the wedding; Albert L. Nichols of East Brookfield, Hammond's fellow-clerk; Charles F. Dunton, Lewis D. Bemis and Charles H. Hobbs. The body was placed in the receiving tomb at the old cemetery, and will be brought to Worcester for burial in Hope Cemetery in the spring.

Among the out-of town relatives were Mr. and Mrs. George Hammond, Mr. and Mrs. Levi Hammond, Mr. and Mrs. Dwight Aldrich all of Charlton.

ONE REPORT

IS PUBLIC!

Another in Secret
to Dist.-Atty. Hoar.

MYSTERY OF SPENCER TRAGEDY DEEPENS

Medical Examiner Keeps
Up Great Silence.

POLITELY POINTS TO WHAT HE HAS WRITTEN.

Official Statement a Puzzle For the Public.

BRUISE AND CUT ON BODY OF
MRS. PROUTY.

Suggestion That Cord Made Mark on Neck.

Special to The Telegram

Spencer. Jan. 10 – Public interest in the sensational suicides of Henry Hammond and Mrs. Maria L. Prouty has not abated in the least and today more wild rumors were afloat than ever. Most sensational reports have been put in circulation, and friends of the sorrowing relatives are aghast at the widespread notoriety which the unhappy double tragedy has involved them.

Medical Examiner Dr. E. W. Norwood today filed his official report with Town Clerk A. W. Curtis and Dist. Atty. Rockwood Hoar, The medical examiner's official findings throw no new light upon the suicides. To some minds the doctor's report of Mrs. Prouty's death makes the case more mysterious than ever.

The sense of the new mystery is called by a sentence in Dr. Norwood's report which refers to a bruise on the left temple of the dead woman, and the infliction of a slight cut upon the right forefinger. Dr. Norwood was seen in his office tonight by reporters, and was courteously asked to throw some light upon these two new facts. The doctor is a busy man, and there were patients waiting for him at the time, but he answered courteously enough, despite the pressure upon his time.

The medical examiner's answers were polite, but emphatic, and he firmly but pleasantly refused to discuss the point in any shape whatever.

"I have made my official report," said Dr. Norwood, "and that comprises all I know. If the district-attorney is dissatisfied, he may take nay action he sees fit. I must refuse to answer any questions."

Despite the fact that Dr. Norwood is medical examiner, no person in Spencer, with proper regard for a physician's professional reserve, blames him for his reticence. Dr. Norwood's position is a most peculiar one, and he is regarded as wholly justifiable in keeping his mouth closed.

In the first place, he is the physician for William H. Prouty and family, and secondly, is a close personal friend of the grief-stricken husband. In his official capacity as medical examiner he has filed his report and right there he claim his duty to the public callers. He is not a friend to sensationalism and in order to hide the wounded feelings of the husband and daughters, he refrains from discussing a case he regards as bad enough already.

Reluctance to tell, on the part of those who know the facts, is the chief factor in keeping alive morbid interest in the sad tragedy.

The medical examiner's report of Henry Hammond's suicide is practically just the same that has been published, and official gives as his opinion that death ensued from a bullet wound, self-inflicted. This is the official report of Mrs. Prouty's death.

Commonwealth of Massachusetts
Worcester, Mass.

Report of a view of the body of a woman whose name is Maria Louise Prouty, 50 years, 9 months, 19 days. Said body was found lying Spencer at 7 o'clock in the afternoon of the 7th day of January, 1899.

The body was lying in bed in bedroom at residence, in clothes which might ordinarily have been worn in afternoon. Rigor mortis had not developed. The extremities were cold, but parts of body and especially abdomen retained animal heat.

Along a line extending from a point about one-half inch below right ear, across throat just above the larynx to similar point below left ear, the skin was discolored and tissues slightly depressed.

The greatest point of depression---perphaps one-sixteenth inch long, directly over the larynx.

This discoloration was from one-eighth to one-fourth inch in width, and the condition such as might have been caused by the pressure of a small, tightly-drawn cord.

The skin of the face was mottled with small, purple spots.

Eyes and mouth were open, but no real distortion of face.

There was a slight bruise on left temple, and slight cut of recent origin on forefinger of right hand.

And I further declare it to be my opinion that the said Maria Louise Prouty came to her death from suicide by strangulation.

E. W. Norwood,
Medical Examiner.

Jan. 7, 1899.

This report is on file at the town clerk's office. The medical examiner's report sent today to Dist.-Atty. Rockwood Hoar was not made public, and nothing is known of its details or character.

There is no exact statement, that Mrs. Prouty hanged herself with a rope in the attic of her home on Ash street.

It is not stated that she strangled herself with a silk handkerchief. It is intimated in the official report that a cord was used, but nothing is said of the way in which Mrs. Prouty used the cord, whether as a garret or as a means of suspending her body by the neck.

Dr. Norwood has frankly said he does not know. He has said he cannot swear where the suicide took place. "The room was very dark," is the way the doctor put it.

When Dr. Norwood first saw the body Saturday night, it lay on a bed. A neighbor had tenderly placed a white cotton handkerchief over the dead face. There was a silk handkerchief around the neck.

The husband of the dead woman discovered the body, as nearly as can be ascertained, in the attic of the Prouty home on Ash street. The attic is a large, bare apartment and takes up all of the space beneath the roof.

Interest in the suicide case received fresh impetus again this afternoon account of one influx of Boston newspaper men. One evening paper three men in town all the afternoon carefully probing for new facts, and industriously going over the ground already covered by The Telegram. Other Boston papers had reporters and an artist here, and at one period this afternoon there were six reporters lined up at the Massasoit.

The delegation of Boston men left Spencer on the 6:22 train on the Boston & Albany railroad, equipped with the biggest array of haphazard rumors and obscure "They-say-so's" that ever went out of Spencer in a bunch. The reporters all agreed that the case is the most mysterious they have ever tackled.

SPENCER HAS THIRD
SINCE NEW YEAR

SUICIDE IS
EPIDEMIC !

CHARLES DUMAS SICK
OF LIFE IN ITS PRIME.

Reputable Workman With
Happy Family Home.

CALMLY HINTS OF HIS FATE

FOR DAYS AHEAD.

Offers to Bet Two Dollars That He Will Succeed.

NO REASON GIVEN EXCEPT CASE OF THE GRIP.

Accentuates Sensation of Preceding Tragedy.

Special to The Telegram

SPENCER, Jan. 20 – Charles Dumas, aged 31 years and 3 days, committed suicide this morning at 5:50 o'clock, by shooting himself, at his home in Upper Wire Village, two miles from the center of Spencer. He is the third Spencer residence to commit suicide since New Years day, and the exclamation is common today that Spencer is becoming a notorious town for suicides.

For the past week Dumas talked with close friends and fellow workmen of killing himself. Tuesday night he said to Alec Boulay, bartender at Napoleon Cabana's saloon:-

"I'm going to be dead Sunday, Alley, and I want you to come to the funeral."

He was watched by his family and a friend most of last night, but early this morning, while his wife was preparing breakfast for the family, he was left alone for a short time, and , taking advantage of this opportunity, sent a bullet into his brain.

He acted with care and deliberation, and almost instantaneous death was the result of his firm pressure on the trigger of the 32-caliber revolver with which he ended his life.

He held the muzzle of the revolver close against his forehead, and the bullet was lodged at the base of the brain. It was exactly two weeks ago this morning that Henry Hammond, son of Aaron & Ida Hammond, took his life close upon the terrible double tragedy of two weeks ago gives greater prominence, and the sad affair has been the sole topic of conversation today in public places.

Dumas, like Henry Hammond, shot himself in the center of the forehead, and at the same time of day a few minutes before 6 o'clock in the morning.

His family and friends are at a lost to known why he took his life. He was always given plenty of work and he made good wages.

Dumas's wife says he was not well for a week prior to the suicide, and attributes the cause to grip.

Dumas was well known in Spencer and he had a host of friends who are unanimous in saying he was a steady workman and a good fellow. He was formerly a member of the Wire village baseball team. In his own precinct, Wire village, he was highly respected.

SUICIDE BY SHOOTING.

Another Tragic Event in Spencer.

CHARLES DUMAS KILLS HIMSELF.

Said to Have Been Drinking heavily

Special Dispatch to The Gazette.

SPENCER, Jan. 20 – Another suicide occurred this morning, when Charles Dumas of Wire Village shot himself through the forehead between the eyes, causing instant death. Dumas is said to have been drinking heavily for the past two weeks. Yesterday he was in Worcester and came home in the afternoon, and several times threatened to commit suicide. Some of his friends stayed with the family all night, and watched him, but Dumas apparently being all right this morning, they left about 6 o'clock, Mrs. Dumas was in the basement, preparing breakfast, and about 6:30 o'clock, hearing a pistol shot, rushed upstairs, to find her husband dead. Medical Examiner Norwood was summoned, and pronounced it a case of suicide. Dumas was about 35 years old, and leaves a widow and three small children. He was employed at the mills of the Spencer Wire Company.

The widow and children of Charles Dumas, the Wire village suicide, will not be paid a dollar of the $600 death benefit allowed to heirs of deceased members by St. Jean Baptiste society. The funeral of the victim was this morning, but the society was not represented at the house, church or grave. An iron-clad bylaw of the society denies all favors to members who die by their own hands. In cases of death by sickness or accident, the widow or orphans of a dead member are paid, $600, or at the rate of $1 for every man in the organization.

Suicide is so strongly abhorred by the society that the constitution makes a special provision, taking away all privileges. Usually a delegation of 50 men of the society escort the body of a member to the grave, but at the funeral of Dumas today no members appeared. There is likely to be a contest made by the widow and brother of the dead man to try the legality of the denial of the death benefit. It is considered by many people in Spencer that Dumas was insane when he shot himself.

Friends of the dead man delegated Napoleon Cabana, a member of St. Jean Baptiste society, to express thanks today to The Telegram for its accurate account of the suicide, and the painstaking way in which The Telegram exploded the erroneous report of other papers, that Dumas was drunk. Mr. Cabana thanked The Telegram today and in bitter terms denounced the malevolent sheet which attacked the reputation of the dead man.

Although it is against the custom of Roman Catholic churches to allow the benefit of the church, Rev. A. A. Lamy, pastor of St. Mary's church, proved superior to prejudice today, and not only celebrated a mass of requiem at the church for the suicide, but also gave permission for burial in consecrated ground. Fr. Lamy takes a charitable view of, Albert Germain, Louis Aegis and Joseph Brigham. Interment was in St. Mary's cemetery.

Napoleon Cabana said today that Dumas told him one day last week that an angel called him the unhappy affair, and inclined to the insanity theory, which leaves Dumas' memory undefiled in church circles.

There was no singing at the service in the church. Many people were curious to see for themselves how a suicide's funeral would be managed, and went to the church at 9 o'clock this morning. The coffin was borne by Julius Wedge, John Brigham, Joseph N. Stone, and told him to die Sunday. This, in Mr. Cabana's opinion, indicates, that Dumas was crazy.

Mrs. Dumas and her children are left destitute, and will have to be supported by the town.

Worcester Telegram-Friday Morning January 27, 1899

HIRES A ROOM

TO KILL HIMSELF

John L. Taylor of Boston Cuts

His Throat in Worcester.

DEED IS DONE AT HOME OF

JOSEPH PAYETTE

Hospital Surgeons Put Him in Shape
to live

John L. Taylor, 55 Temple street, Boston, cut his throat with a razor in the home of Joseph Payette, 13 Millbury street, at 8 o'clock last night.

He was taken to the city hospital in police ambulance, and this morning the doctors thought he would recover. His throat was cut in three places, and his windpipe was severed. He is 63 years old and has a wife, who lives at 55 Temple street, Boston.

Taylor is thought to be a commercial trader, it is not known when he came to Worcester, but yesterday afternoon at 3:50 o'clock he went to the home of Mr. Payette, and asked if he could engage a room.

The Payette family cannot talk English well, but through a woman who lives downstairs, they and Taylor were able to reach an agreement. He asked how much they would charge for a week, and on being told $2, he inquired the cost for three days. He was told he could have it for $1, and paid the money.

When Mrs. Payette offered to clean the room and make some improvements in it, Taylor smiled and said, "never mind. It is all right for my purpose."

He went out when he had completed his arrangements with the Payettes and remained 20 minutes. On his return he entered the bathroom, remained in it half an hour, and left it just in time to prevent the family making an investigation. They say he went directly to his room from the bathroom, and they did not see him again until they and Horace Beaudette, a visitor, heard a fall in Taylor's room.

Beaudette pushed the door open, and Taylor was lying on the floor in a pool of blood. A razor lay between his legs, but he was not moaning or making any effort to call anyone.

Beaudette asked him what was the matter, but the only reply he could get from Taylor was a request to be allowed to go to the bathroom. Beaudette thought he was dying, and instead placed him on the bed and ran for a doctor.

He found Dr. J. M. Steele in his office, 183 Green street. Soon after he and the doctor reached the house Sergt. William Hickey and Officers George H. Davis and David J. Whalen of station 2 arrived.

Taylor had lost considerable blood, but was conscious, and asked the doctor to allow him to go to the bathroom. The doctor refused and asked him why he had tried to end his life.

"Let me go to the bathroom and when I come back I will tell you all about it," was his reply.

Sergt. Hickey telephoned for the police ambulance, and Dr. Steele bound cloths around Taylor's throat. He did not think he could live, but when he reached the hospital the doctors went rapidly to work upon him and stopped the flow of blood.

They found he had hacked his throat three times, inflicting the most jagged wounds they had seen for months, and had made a hole in his windpipe that would have killed him had he remained much longer without surgical attention.

The doctors put several stitches in the windpipe and the other cuts, and if something they do not anticipate does not happen Taylor will be all right in a short time.

Taylor would not tell any one at the hospital why he attempted his life, but told Sergt. Hickey before he was taken from the Payette house he was despondent.

Sergt. Hickey thinks Taylor came to Worcester and engaged the room in the Payette residence with deliberate intention of committing suicide.

The razor he used, and his pocketbook, containing a number of papers, are in the possession of Sergt. Hickey. In the pocketbook was a promissory note for $100, drawn by the Malden Carriage Co., and payable to Stewart Bros., in two months. The note is indorsed by Taylor and was made a few weeks ago.

There is a receipt from the First M. E. church of Boston for a subscription of $7 paid by Taylor and his wife, a receipt for dues from Landmark lodge, I. O. O. F., one from West End club for payment for a room, one showing that he gave his note Oct. 31,1898, for $225 to the heirs of Samuel Guild, and signed by George F. Child, and several other cards and personal papers.

He had not said what business he is engaged in, but told the Payettes when he talked with them about a room he was not looking for a position, as he had one in Boston. He told them he arrived in Worcester a short time before from New York.

Several of the letters found in his pocket are addressed to him at 28 Sudbury street, Boston. He did not ask that his wife be notified and no word has been sent to her.

DEATH TAKES HIM AT HIS INTENT

John L. Taylor, Who Cut His Throat, Dies at City Hospital.

WIFE AND DAUGHTER IN BOSTON NOT SURPRISED.

Stepson in Worcester Says He Had More Money.

John L. Taylor of Boston, who cut his throat with a razor Thursday night in the tenement of Joseph Payette, 13 Millbury street, died at City hospital a few minutes to 1 o'clock this morning.

The doctors thought Thursday that they would be able to save his life, but he began to grow weak yesterday afternoon, and last night they saw that he could not recover. His body will be sent to Boston for interment.

A. M. Pease, a stepson of Taylor, came to Worcester yesterday from Boston, and talked with him at City hospital. Pease told the hospital authorities Taylor had been despondent for some time and he told Chief of Police James M. Drennan before he went to the hospital that he has had trouble in business.

It was expected that he would end his life and when the news of his attempt at suicide was told his wife and daughter in their home at 55 Temple street, Boston, yesterday, they did not seem surprised.

Taylor was 63 years old and leaves wife and daughter. He had one son and a stepson, Pease.

Taylor was the proprietor of the Dun's stitching works at 28 Sudbury street, Boston, and was formerly well-to-do. Chief of Police Drennan has his pocketbook containing his papers and $2.35. His stepson was much surprised yesterday when he learned that was all the money Taylor had, and asked the chief if he had any idea what could have become of a good deal more Taylor was thought to have had.

STABS IN BODY MANGLED ON RAIL.

Spencer's Specter of Death Follows a Man Out West.

FR. DOLAN STIRS PEOPLE BY TEMPERANCE TALK.

Special to The Telegram

SPENCER, Jan.28 – *Francois X. Berry of Holyoke, formerly a resident of Spencer, was murdered Friday at Pass Christian, Miss., and details of the crime have not yet been sent to his home. The murdered man worked in the Isaac Prouty & Co. shoe shop three years ago. Nelson Berry of 5 Pond street and Joseph E. Berry of Adams street are relatives of the dead man.*

News of the crime has not been sent to Berry's old home in Holyoke, as the authorities who today were making inquiries were at sea as to the man's place of residence. Berry's body was picked up early Saturday morning on the tracks of the Louisville & Nashville railroad at Pass Christian, horribly mangled by trains that passed in the night. He had been stabbed in the throat and breast, and there was evidence to indicate that a coupling pin had been used to batter in his skull, although actual proof of this is wanting on account of the mutilation of the body by the cars.

C. N. Kendall, chief of police of North Adams, got word yesterday that a man named Frank Berry had been murdered at Pass Christian. Chief Kendall put his officers to work in North Adams to locate relatives, but none were found. The chief's informant of the tragedy was Charles H. Tornton of Pass Christian, a reputable man, who had sat on the coroner's jury to inquire into Berry's death. From remarks which Berry made in a saloon in Pass Christian, Thursday, overheard by others, the jury was led to believe that the murdered man belonged in North Adams. This, however, is not so, Berry probably worked there a short time, long enough to obtain impressions of the town and talk about places he remembered there.

Chief Kendall naturally was at sea in quest for Berry's folks. He may have sent inquiries to Holyoke.

Berry was in a saloon in the little Mississippi city late Friday night, drinking with two other men. The three men were seen to leave the saloon together. When Berry's body was found, it was at first thought that he had fallen victim of an accident on the tracks, but direct stab wounds were noted in his throat and chest, which even mutilation of the car wheels did not conceal. The supposition is that Berry was murdered and his body was put on the tracks at night in order that trains might mangle the body beyond hope of recognition or discovery of crime. There was nothing found on the body by which identity might be established. People who viewed the corpse recognized in it the man who had been drinking in a saloon, had mentioned North Adams, Mass., and had left in company with two other men. The men who left the saloon with Berry have been found and arrested. The findings of the coroner's jury was that Berry was probably murdered and his body placed on the railroad to cover up the crime.

There are several Berry families in Holyoke, Nelson Berry of 5 Pond street is working there in the wool yard of Pierre Berry, a relative. Joseph E. Berry, when seen for The Telegram today, was not able to say definitely to which branch of the family the dead man belonged, but he recognized the name and general description, and thinks Frank Berry was a cousin.

SPENCER. – Relatives of Francois X. Berry attempted today to learn more details of the murder of the young man, an account of which was published in The Telegram today. Nelson L. Berry, son of Nelson Berry, 5 Pond street, who is working in Holyoke for Pierre Berry wrote today to his father to ascertain more particulars. Nelson L. Berry is of the opinion that the man who was murdered in Pass Christian, Miss., is a cousin of his fathers.

128

Kingsley
Funeral Home Ledge   Oct 17

Miss Ratigan

Paid   To 1 Bench   13.00

To J & W Temple   4.50

Mrs Erastus Jones
To Meeting die Matt   1.50
" Hair   80
" Making our 1 Class   60
" 2½ Wheli Hair   90

Mrs Catherine Myrick
To 20 Springs   1.00
" Burlap   50
Paid " Tacks & twine   35
" Webbing Curbued Wadding   87
" 3⅓ yds Covering   16.67
" 6 yds Fring   12.00
" Labor   6.00 $37.?

Geo P DeWolf
To left Chair   1.98

E Harris Howland
To left Sleigh   2.90
2.00

Paid   Super Joff 3
To Mrs   5.12

21st
Est of Henry Hammund
For Casket & Box   45.00

138   January 5—   1899

J. Routy & Co.   1 Paige

John J. Griffen

Funeral Expenses

Adam Hammond
To 1 Basket & Box   125.00
  "   Laying out & Embalming   5.00
  "   Hearse & Attendance   4.00
Paid "   Shaving   2.00
  "   Chairs   5 dz   2.50
  "   Carriages   18.00
  "   Singing   6.00
  "   Care of Teams   1.25   162.75
  "   Mr. Bronze   1.00

11   William Routy
To 1 Basket & Box   60.00
  "   Embalming   4.00
  "   Hearse & Attendance   4.00
  5   Carriages   15.00
  "   1 dz Chairs   .50
  "   Opening Grave   4.00   87

GEORGE F. McKENNA EXPIRES SUDDENLY

Suffers Collapse Soon After Having Entered Corridor of Main-St. Building

George F. McKenna, 62, of 7 Monroe avenue, widely known in this city and formerly proprietor of the Commercial hotel on Front street, died suddenly in the lobby of the State Mutual building, shortly after 9 o'clock today.

Mr. McKenna had just entered the building and was waiting for an elevator, when he suddenly collapsed.

The ambulance, with Police Surgeon Richard J. Shannahan, responded to an emergency call, but Mr. McKenna was dead when Dr. Shannahan arrived.

Death was attributed to a heart attack.

The body was removed to the City hospital morgue and relatives notified.

Mr. McKenna came to Worcester from Spencer, where he served at one time as chief of police. For several years he was a traveling salesman for the Worcester Brewing Co. He was also proprietor of the Hotel Franklin on Mal street, taking over control of that house on the death of Patrick H. Hurley.

Mr. McKenna leaves his wife, Mary E. (Deedy) McKenna, and a brother, Henry.

Date of Death 1-0-99

DOB 12-19-76

Dec 19 1875

Commonwealth of Massachusetts.

No. ___

RETURN OF A DEATH.

To the Clerk of the City or Town in which the death occurred.

(FILL OUT WITH INK. ALL NAMES TO BE IN FULL.)

Name, *Henry Hammond*   Sex, *Male*   Color, *White*

Date of Death, *Jan 6th* 189 *9*; Age, *23* Years, Months, *18* Days.

Maiden Name, { If married, widowed } ___

Husband's Name, ___

Single, Married, Widowed or Divorced, *Single*   Occupation, *clerk*

*Residence, { If out of town, also state fully, } *Spencer Mass*

Place of Birth, *Worcester Mass*

*Place of Death, *Spencer Mass*

Name of Father, *Aaron Hammond*

Birthplace of Father, *Charlton Mass*

Maiden name of Mother, *J. L. Snow*

Birthplace of Mother, *Worcester*

Place of Interment, (Give name of Cemetery), ___

Dated at *Spencer* ___ 189 *9*   Signature and place of business of Undertaker, { *A E Kingsley* *Main St Spencer Mass* }

on *Jan 6th*

PHYSICIAN'S CERTIFICATE.

Name and Age of Deceased,† *Henry Hammond* Age *23* Y M *18* D

Place and Date of Death,‡ died at *Spencer January 6th* 189 *9*

Disease or Cause of Death,§ *Suicide*

Duration of sickness, *Immediate Death*

I certify that the above is true to the best of my knowledge and belief.

Signature and Residence { of Certifying Physician } *E W Norwood* M. D. *Spencer Mass*

Date of Certificate, *January 6th* 189 *9*

Give also street and number, if any.
† Or sex of infant not named. If still-born, so state. ‡ If child died immediately after birth, so state.
§ If a Soldier or Sailor in the War of the Rebellion, give both Primary and Secondary Cause.

245

Date of Decar 1-7-99
D.O.B. April, 19-1848

Commonwealth of Massachusetts.

No.

RETURN OF A DEATH.

To the Clerk of the City or Town in which the death occurred.

(FILL OUT WITH INK. ALL NAMES TO BE IN FULL.)

Name, *Maria L Prouty*   Sex, _____ Color, _____

Date of Death, *January 7th* 189*9*; Age, *50* Years, *9* Months, *19* Days.

Maiden Name, {If married, widowed or divorced} *Maria L Peel*

Husband's Name, *William H Prouty*

Single, Married, Widowed or Divorced, *Married* Occupation, _____

*Residence, {If out of town, also state fully.} *Spencer*

Place of Birth, *Leicester*

*Place of Death, *Spencer*

Name of Father, *Joseph Peel*

Birthplace of Father, *England*

Maiden name of Mother, *Deputin*

Birthplace of Mother, *Vermont*

Place of Interment, (Give name of Cemetery). *Pine Grove Cemetery Spencer*

Dated at *Spencer*
on *Jan 7th* 189*9*

Signature and place of business of Undertaker. { *A H Kingsley*
Main St Spencer }

PHYSICIAN'S CERTIFICATE.

Name and Age of Deceased,† *Maria Louise Prouty* Age, *50* Y. *9* M. *19* D.

Place and Date of Death,‡ died at *Spencer Jan. 7* 189*9*

Disease or Cause of Death,§ *Suicide*

Duration of sickness,

I certify that the above is true to the best of my knowledge and belief.

E W Norwood M. D.

Signature and Residence of Certifying Physician. { *Spencer* }

Date of Certificate, *Jan. 7th* 189*9*.

Give also street and number, if any.
† Or sex of infant not named. If still-born, so state. ‡ If child died immediately after birth, so state.
§ If a Soldier or Sailor in the War of the Rebellion, give both Primary and Secondary Cause.

246

Charles Demers Death Certified

Hour of Death 1-20-11

Commonwealth of Massachusetts.

No. 1

RETURN OF A DEATH.

To the Clerk of the City or Town in which the death occurred.

(FILL OUT WITH INK. ALL NAMES TO BE IN FULL)

Name, *Charles Demers*   Sex, *Male* Color, *Wh*

Date of Death, *Jan 20* 189*9*, Age, *31* Years, _____ Months, *2* Days.

Maiden Name, {If married, widowed or divorced.} _____

Husband's Name, _____

Single, Married, Widowed or Divorced *Married* Occupation, *Wire puller*

*Residence, {If out of town, also state fully.} *Spencer*

Place of Birth, *Canada*

*Place of Death, *Spencer*

Name of Father, *Francoisse Demers*

Birthplace of Father, *Canada*

Maiden name of Mother, *Taize Bonin*

Birthplace of Mother, *Canada*

Place of Interment, (Give name of Cemetery). *Spencer - St. Mary's*

Dated *Spencer* } *E. F. Amelotte*

on *Jan 20* 189*9* Signature and place of business of Undertaker. { *Spencer mas*

PHYSICIAN'S CERTIFICATE.

Name and Age of Deceased,† *Charles J. Demers* Age, *31* Y., M. *2* D.

Place and Date of Death,‡ died at *Spencer Mass Jan 20* 189*9*

Disease or Cause of Death,§ *suicide*

Duration of sickness, _____

I certify that the above is true to the best of my knowledge and belief.

Signature and Residence of Certifying Physician. { *C. A. Norwood Medex* M. D.

Spencer

Date of Certificate, *Jan 20* 189*9*.

Give also street and number, if any.
† Or sex of infant not named. If still-born, so state.   ‡ If child died immediately after birth, so state.
§ If a Soldier or Sailor in the War of the Rebellion, give both Primary and Secondary Cause.

247